The erotic education of a Lady of Pleasure, told in letters to her granddaughter.

Sweet Fanny

edited and illustrated by
Faye Rossignol

HEADLINE

Copyright © Faye Rossignol 1989

First published in Great Britain in 1989
by HEADLINE BOOK PUBLISHING PLC

All rights reserved. No part of this publication may be
reproduced, stored in a retrieval system, or transmitted,
in any form or by any means without the prior written
permission of the publisher, nor be otherwise circulated
in any form of binding or cover other than that in which
it is published and without a similar condition being
imposed on the subsequent purchaser.

All characters in this publication are fictitious
and any resemblance to real persons, living or dead,
is purely coincidental.

ISBN 0 7472 3275 X

Typeset in 10/12¼ pt Plantin
by Colset Pte Ltd, Singapore

Printed and bound in Great Britain by
Collins, Glasgow

HEADLINE BOOK PUBLISHING PLC
Headline House
79 Great Titchfield Street
London W1P 7FN

Sweet Fanny

LETTER ONE

FROM MOUNT VENUS,
Wednesday, February 20th, 1850

Sweet Fanny,

No! I shall not say it again – no, no, a thousand times NO. You and your dear mother have had your last penny from me. If we go on as we are, you will bankrupt me between you.

We have never spoken of it, but you realize, I'm sure, how I earned my fortune. From the time I was sixteen until the age of thirty-two, I 'spread the gentlemen's relish', as the saying goes. In short, I was a Lady of Pleasure. Now a Lady of Pleasure is like the squirrel, she covers her back with her tail. But I copied the squirrel in another way, too, for I saved it all – some ninety thousand guineas or more, for I never parted my thighs under two guineas, and often got a great deal more. Gentlemen had to spend *on* me if they wished to spend *in* me. But my daughter, your dear mother, somewhere acquired (and I fear she has passed it on to you) a taste in living that would run away with it all in half that number of years.

It shall not happen. I, who am now fifty, was born with this century and I propose to see it out – *with my capital undiminished*. So, if you wish to continue in your enjoyment of fine clothes, carriages, servants, and good food (or what passes for it in England these days), you must either marry this odious old lord your mother has found for you, or you will have to get up off your fortune and earn it in the good old way. If you marry, then his lordship will provide for your mother; if you take up the Old Game, then I shall help you maintain her.

Ah me! What a choice! You must think it dreadful, I'm sure. But 'tis not so. Consider only this: Ld D. is a crapulous old Toad, and no sweet young girl of sixteen could feel anything but revulsion for him. If you marry him, you are obliged to open your thighs beneath him every night; then you accept all the worst that goes with the Old Game, while experiencing none of its joys. And believe me, it has joys in plenty – more, perhaps, than is good for the passionate young female I see in you. The men call us Ladies of Pleasure, meaning a Pleasure that is theirs; yet I have come all to pieces with that same Pleasure more often than they, I dare swear. Not a day passed in all those sixteen years that I did not crack and rejoice at least once, and usually more often.

To put it starkly: you may grant the Favour of your Sweet Young Body as often as Ld D. may require it and get no Pleasure in return, or you may share the Enjoyment of your Charms with as many fine gentlemen as you could desire, find more Pleasure in it than you ever thought possible, and have the poor creatures pay *you* for enjoying *them*!

Consider this as well: When you are broken-in to the occupation, your little Centre of Bliss can stand the traffic of five or six strong thrusters a day without hurt. (I once did thirty-five on an occasion I may yet tell you of but had to resort to other Tricks for some days thereafter.) If you avoid drink and other strong stimulants, you will be able to ask five guineas of each. And do not think it ends there. My fee was never anything but my fee – a charge of entrance that did not cover the buffet or the bar; so when the feast was done, and I had sighed and trembled and fell all to pieces with my Lover, I would ask him breathlessly, 'Was I not *splendid*? Did you ever enjoy such Voluptuary Abandon in your life?' And, since Men's memories are as short as they think their ramrods long, they would say, 'Why no . . . 'pon my life . . . I never remember it so rewarding as that . . .' And so forth – No, let me rephrase that. Do not think me cynical of Men. I love them all and would enjoy the most of them again if I had my time over.

Let me put it thus – When a Man has found *rare* Pleasure with a girl, he is in a soft and melting mood with her. Poor Man – the Pleasure would be more common if whores' characters were less so. Most of our so-called Ladies of Joy are nothing of the sort. Ladies of Vacant Minds and Leather Pussies would be a truer terminology; for they lie on their backs and count stars or dream of their Fancy Men and wait in idleness for the jigajig to finish. No wonder they need Fancy Men to console them, who take all their earnings and give them nothing but a Pleasure they could as easily find in their trade if they but sought it there.

But what was I saying? Ah yes – no wonder, too, that poor Men are so overwhelmed when they find a torrent of Pleasure in what they thought was yet another hack; and in those tender moments your five guineas can easily be wheedled into ten – and certainly, on average, seven. (I use modern figures, suitable to the general rise in prosperity; in my day it was more like three guineas to be wheedled up to five. But then a Covent Garden blowsabella would do it for fourpence who would ask a shilling now. So all is relative.) Anyway, three guineas or five, the important thing is to agree the fee at the start but to refuse all payment until it is done. (A common Bankside bangtail would throw up her hands in horror at this; they want the cash to be down before they will follow it. I speak only of my own genteel practice as a Lady of Pleasure.) So when it is done, when you have given your paying Lover the thrill and delight of his life and he is still panting with it, lying at your side in wonder, when he agrees: 'I never remember it so rewarding *etc*.' – then it is time to drop a hint or two. Example: 'Oh, my darling Man, (gasp, gasp) I hope there are no more Lovers like you down there, waiting to fetch me up here to bed, for I declare – one more such Taste of Bliss and I shall be dead for the night. Then who will pay the bailiff, eh? I declare – Lovers like you will be the ruin of me.' *Et cetera, et cetera*.

I kept a book always, with a page for each Lover wherein I noted not only his name (as he gave it me), appearance, size of Member, special needs and dislikes, time taken, fee gained – but also, most important, what verbal conversation we had enjoyed and what Wheedle I had used to augment the agreed fee. I cannot tell you the number of Lovers who have said to me, 'I know I am special to you . . . you do not make me feel I frigged a whore . . . you remember so many particular things about me . . .' and so forth. And yet if I passed them in the street 'twas not discretion that kept me from recognizing them. And it was all thanks to my Book of Paradise, as I called it. I shall tell you more of this anon, if you fall in with my plans for your future.

I did not complete my mathematics. You will usually trade three weeks without pause and rest one, while the Cardinal pays his monthly call. 'Tis too crude to multiply $7 \times 6 \times 21$ and get 882 guineas as your monthly income. Ascot does not wait upon your Cardinal, nor does Jenny Lind at the Opera. Nor does that Lover with whom you fall truly and deeply in love – which, if your heart is as weak and susceptible as mine, will happen all too often. Yet withal you should see at least 800 guineas each month. Thus you will earn the best part of ten thousand guineas a year, of which you will spend but two (thus living at four times your present highly extravagant rate, by the way).

Sweet Fanny, can this even be called 'a choice'?

Say at least that you will consider it. Your dear mother, I know, has brought you up to hate our Family Trade and will have set your mind most unnaturally against it. What does she suppose pays for *her* fine clothes, *her* carriages, *her* house and servants, and so forth? But no, I am harsh to blame her entirely, for it was I who chose, in my folly, to bring her up in ignorance of the truth – never for one moment imagining that the fatuous oaf you were taught to call your father would so poison her mind.

So, Sweet Child, set aside that stupid prejudice and tell me *your* mind is not poisoned, too. Then I shall write to

5

you further, recalling what I can of the Life and passing on such advice as I have distilled from my years as a Lady of Pleasure.

Ever yours, sweet nymph,
Frances
Comtesse de C.

LETTER TWO

FROM MOUNT VENUS,
Wednesday, 6th March, 1850

Sweet Fanny,

How happy you have made your old Grandmama. I wept with joy to read you will at least *consider* taking up the Gay Old Life rather than shivering nightly in Ld D.'s disgusting bed. Well done! That is splendid sense!

But, dear child, what gloomy questions you ask! And what terrible fears for one so young and sweet to entertain! Such thoughts did not cross my mind until I was well broken to the Trade. So that is where I shall deal with them in answering you – i.e. some letters hence. To deal with such a dismal catalogue now would, I am sure, put you off the whole Business entirely. So pardon me if I answer in my own good time. I have not forgot them, rest assured.

First I must hark back to something I said in my previous letter, where I spoke of spreading the Gentlemen's Relish some ten thousand times betwixt the ages of sixteen and thirty-two. What a loose and wanton Woman you must now think me! For I neglected to add that I did not mean I lay with ten thousand *different gentlemen*! God save the mark but I was never so Lewd as that! No, on my oath, I swear I never parted my thighs for more than *one* thousand individual Persons – fifteen hundred at the most. For every Lover who enjoyed my Favour once and never came again (or not into me), there were a dozen for whom a hundred Ecstasies were not enough. So do not think your old Grannie as dissolute and promiscuous as her vaunting makes her seem, sweet child.

Well, then – where to begin? If I ever set down my memoirs, I suppose I should start in the usual way – my Pranks with the gardener's boy, my Lascivious Experiments with my father's curate, our Discovery and Undoing, my Running Away, and my ineffable good fortune at meeting the Comte de C. who found me at sixteen and taught me how to enter that Land of Inexpressible Pleasure, which no woman can discover on her own – and who found me again at thirty-two with my Passport to it still valid and at last did me the honour he wished he had done me the day we met. (However, *entre nous, ma chère*, I am glad he did not get *his* ring on *my* finger so early – 'twas the other way about, in fact. For I truly believe no woman now living has enjoyed more of Life and Men than I. I think back with eternal gratitude to the hundreds of Gentlemen who have Pleasur'd me and paid me well for their Privilege. And now the dear Comte is all of them in one; and his One is me! But I wander.)

No. These are no memoirs in that sense. If you wish to

read such things I am sending you by a trustworthy fellow just such an autobiography, a famous book called *Fanny Hill*. It was a gift to me from the Comte, in the days of my tutelage, and it helped wash the dust of hypocrisy from my eyes. The identity of the name Fanny and the fact that my maiden name was *Dale*, only added to my sense of kinship with young Miss Hill. I hope it will do the same for you in every way.

So, if this letter and those that follow are not strictly a memoir, what may one call the work? Think of it as a kind of Tourist, or *Vade Mecum*, to guide you into the Peaks of Voluptuousness and Desire. You ask me to describe for you one Occasion of Joy with *one* Lover that will in some way serve for them all. Alas, Sweet Child, 'tis an impossibility. The very essence of your Life of Pleasure lies in its variety. So, if you will permit me to adapt your request, I will tell you not of one Encounter but of one particular night – which has always stuck in my mind, and for reasons which you shall shortly understand.

I was then nineteen and well broken to the Trade. Your mother had not turned two years of age and was boarded with dear old Mrs Fennel in Tunbridge Wells. You will find it hard to picture me as I was then, but try. I was on the tall side, but not by very much. Also I carried less fat than was then the fashion. (If you decide upon the Life, you would also be well advised to regulate your weight, for I have noticed that those who promise *pneumatic* bliss are more prone to female troubles than those of us who traded under less ample flags.) My hair was then as black as a raven's wing, with the same magical sheen of blue; it was also wonderfully luxuriant and reached below my waist when I or my Lovers set it free. (A doctor I once knew sneered at this but I swear there is something in Men's milt that a woman may absorb through the soft walls of her *Love Canal* and that adds a special lustre to her hair and skin. That is why most Ladies of Pleasure have such fine heads and why Old Maids would do better wearing pot scourers for wigs. Anyway, that is my opinion.) My parsley, too, as we call the shrubbery around the Furrows of Venus, had that same jet colour with its sheen of blue. Gentlemen have told me that its promise of darkness and mystery – hiding my little Miss Laycock with hints of electric thrills – added greatly to my charms; and I have always pitied girls of fairer colour whose pale parsley half-reveals that cleft which should only be opened to view when the feast is well under way.

However, there I was, embarking upon young womanhood, in full vigour of life, strong and lusty, adventurous, athirst for novelty, sure of my powers over Men, and in the full flower of my physical charms. My face had that fine-boned structure which has served me so well to this present day. High, wide cheekbones, which always promise generosity in a woman . . . dark, limpid eyes which, without effort on my part, hinted at sympathy and understanding and so prompted confessions and requests that were denied to many a girl with eyes that were superficially more pretty yet somehow cool. No Man ever knew what I truly felt for him, whether I broke with Joy upon him or merely gave the outward show of it (which was, of course, more often the case); but when he gazed deep into my eyes, he *thought* he knew. And that, too, has its price.

My nose was as patrician then as 'tis now. No Lover, looking at its superior line, would think of bilking me his fee. My upper lip was as Cupid's Bow, which you will see in the prints by Rowlandson which I shall send you with that same trusty courier; it promised Love and Pleasures of an entirely ethereal kind. My lower lip, however, was

10

full and generous to a fault. It did not contradict the upper but rather complemented it, offering Pleasures of every Sensual degree. Together with my eyes it encouraged my Lovers to whisper their innermost desires in almost certain hope of fulfilment.

I say *almost* certain because, adventurous as I might have been, I was not of that hackney breed that will surrender all dignity and self-respect for a fee. But even when I drew the line, I could lick my lips and flutter my eyelashes with the promise that what I would permit would go far beyond his tawdry fancying.

All this, by the by, is not my own vanity speaking. I assure you, I paraphrase in the most modest terms the extravagant praises Lovers have showered upon me during my gay years – and have given me proof of in the number of times they paid to possess me.

My neck, to proceed with this Inventory of Charms, was long and slender with delicate cups by my collar bones – which, for some reason, Men loved to plant with kisses. My breasts were soft but firm and well-rounded, not as large as many in my Calling. This was not the disadvantage it may seem. Men claim to like large 'dairies', but when a girl so blessed (if that is the word) lies on her back, they flatten like jellyfish and become too diffuse to hold in the hand. And then the men are not so pleased and they knead away in futile attempts to gather it up, which is no Pleasure to either partner. I should like a guinea for every Lover who has told me how delightful it was to be able, during his final thrusts (for that is when they put you on your back), to caress me entire and to run his hand down to my hips and my curvaceous little *derrière* without fear of losing my breast when he ran back up again. Also, my nipples are rather larger than usual, occupying what, on an archery target, would be the 'inner and outer' circles (with the knob that once gave your dear mother suck as the 'bull'); and, to my great good fortune, they harden at the slightest provocation, even when I myself am not especially Excited – which has permitted me to increase my Lovers' pleasures even when they have been unable to do as much for me. (For Men all take it as the sure and certain sign of Absolute Abandon in a woman that her nipples go hard. However, when one thinks of the Proofs of Excitement in *their* bodies, the error is not so amazing.)

My hips were firm and fine, not, as I have said already, encumbered with great rolls of fat. And this, I think, has contributed much to my Pleasure down the years. One of my Lovers, Professor G., Head of the Anatomy Department at G–'s, who professed his love of *my* anatomy almost every week, and sometimes twice a week, for five full years until he died, told me our sensations are in our nerves; so it stands to reason that if they are insulated from our skin by layers of lard, then it is the difference between hearing a fine tenor voice in the same room or muffled through stout walls and velvet curtains and Lord knows what. Often, when I have shivered and gasped in the throes of that Ultimate Joy with a Lover, I have pitied our fat sisters for what will always pass them by.

Touching Prof. G. (which I often did!), many and many a time after we had slaked our Lust, did he take looking glass and candle and give me lessons in my own anatomy – especially of that part which our feminine modesty usually hides from insolent gaze. Or *those parts*, I should say; for down there in Cupid's Furrow is an entire landscape for discovery, and in which, with dear G.'s help, I learned to take as much interest as did the most avid and curious Lover I ever had.

I refer, of course, to little Miss Laycock. She has a hundred other names, which I shall tell you anon if it seems you are warming to the Trade. (Ditto the Horn of

Pleasure and the Act of Delight they make between them. For the present I shall call them . . . oh, whatever comes to mind at the time.) Let me tell you something of the wonder of Miss Laycock. I know it may cause you unease, for, in any other circumstances, it would be a perverse grandmother indeed who even hinted to her virgin granddaughter that such a Commodity exists. But, if you are to take up the Trade, or even consider doing so, then Miss Laycock will become the very heart and soul of your world.

It often struck me as extraordinary that the Thing we sell is really nothing. I mean, it is no *thing*. It is empty air – a space, a hole. When a Loving Man thrusts away in there, he does not actually get *inside* us! I could not believe it, yet Prof. G. assured me it is, indeed, so. That most Intimate and Secret skin of all is no different in any fundamental manner from the skin of our hands. From which it follows that a Lover who imagines himself privileged beyond his dreams to let his Proud Tool explore the darkest recesses of Hairyfordshire, is, in reality, no more inside us than if we took him in hand! It is true! I have the country's foremost anatomist to vouch for it! And I can tell you – the thought has occasionally been a great comfort to me in my worst moments. (And you shall hear of them, too, for I shall hide nothing by the time I'm done.)

So – our Glorious Commodity is nothing but an emptiness. How can one sell nothing? How can one even make nothing look attractive? The answer is: We sell that which *surrounds* our nothingness – the oyster-folds of pearly flesh, the lips within lips, the little hooded rosebud where so much of our Pleasure resides, and the Hole itself, soft, collapsed, puckered in a begging kiss to the great knob that will thrust it apart and iron out every crease . . . and the snug, warm, unseen flesh within, rough before, smooth behind, all to a purpose, as you shall hear. (For the moment, however, I abjure you – take a mirror and candle as you wish and make what discoveries you will, but do not explore beyond your hymeneal gate. Destroy that and you will bleed a hundred guineas for no purpose whatever.)

I shall say more of Miss Laycock anon, but that, at least, is the surrounding, the dressing, of the empty Hole we sell. We may also prink her out with frills and furbelows, to be sure; but for the moment I speak only of her natural adornments. Fortunately, dear randy old Mother Nature has already done nine-tenths of our work for us. Darling G. often begged me to attend his lectures on intimate female anatomy, 'that my students may examine the most perfect specimen I have ever seen'. But I always said they could acquire the knowledge in the usual way – and pay the usual fee – if he but gave them my directions. I asked him in what way I was so perfect, of course. He said my outer lips and inner lips were exactly the right size and distance from each other, so that when the larger ones are parted fully (which is a thing Men love to do and gaze and gaze until you could sometimes fall asleep yourself), the inner ones yield up only the merest glimpse of the Holey of Holeys, and must then be parted too for another eternal session of ocular Adoration. And their colour is pale and delicate – and somehow yielding, or so he swore. My *Miss Fawcett*, as the lesser hole is called, is delicate and small, inviting no unauthorized penetration, nor even permitting a bungled one. And the little rosebud that crowns her forehead is, in me, angled out upon the bone in such a manner that men of every size and shape have little difficulty in bringing her Delight – whether they mean to or no.

And that was your grandmother at nineteen. I had been parted from the Comte and his son two years, one of which had been my lying-in and my resting up after your dear mother's birth; the other I had spent as the mistress not of one Gentleman but of a club of thirty-five. (There were five of us females to slake their Lust, I hasten to add, from little Jenny, who was sixteen to Old Mother Merry, who was sixty. But it is too complicated to describe here. Perhaps another time.) Anyway, I had just left the Other White's, as that club was called, and gone to work for Mrs Featherstonehaugh, who was the proprietress of The Ladies' Academy in Albemarle Street. I did not admire the name *Academy*, for it suggested Discipline, which is a particular branch of our Trade and one I have never liked; but the name was by then well established and Mrs F. would not change. In most ways it was a regular House of Delight, but it had some distinctions of its own.

In the first place, no *whore* ever worked there. I have never considered myself a whore. I am a Lady of Pleasure, with the stress to fall on the Lady. We were all Ladies there at Mrs Featherstonehaugh's. I, as you know, was the daughter of a vicar, himself of a cadet branch of the Earl of S–f–d's family; there were two other daughters of clergymen like me; also several whose fathers were failed merchants, and other girls, too, of the same general rank in society. All of us had excellent educations and were full of accomplishments – quite apart from those of Venus. Also, it may astonish you to hear, we had numbers of married ladies, some of them titled, who spread the relish one or two nights a week, mostly for their own Pleasure but also for profit and 'socket money', as they call it. These latter made the bulk of the girls who worked *in* the academy. We who had no other occupation but to be Occupied as often as possible by Men, were usually employed (as proper young ladies ought to be employed) in Charitable Visits – comforting the afflicted and needy in their own homes. In our case, the Affliction was

15

Overwhelming Desire, the Need was for a sweet young feminine body to slake it; and in that sort of Comfort we were all well practised.

I had been there, as I say, a little above a week, working mostly in the Academy, where we sat looking demure, doing our embroidery or playing the piano and singing sweetly. We would converse daintily with our gentlemen callers until one or other of them could contain his Longing no further and would take us upstairs. Never a Lewd word or gesture was permitted downstairs, so we attracted a very discerning and pleasant class of Lover – Men who would be (or had already been) nauseated by the disgusting sort of banter that passes for wit in the typical whorehouse.

I liked it well enough but there was soon a sort of deadening sameness about my room, the ceiling, and the succession of naked men who disposed my thighs to their liking and then pressed me into the mattress. So I made so bold as to ask Mrs Featherstonehaugh when I might expect a little extramural employment.

'Why, child,' she replied with a laugh. 'You shall enjoy it this very night. Snatch what slumber you can this afternoon, for I swear to you – twixt supper and dawn you shall not rest.'

I felt myself grow a little excited at her promise for I wondered what Hercules she already had me coupled to. (He, you remember, got with child the fifty daughters of Thespius, King of Thespis, and all in a single night!) But, as I might have guessed – for I have only ever met one man who can keep it up all night, and I am married to *him* – it was not one Lover but several.

'You are to go,' she said, 'to the good ship HMS D, which lies at Chatham, and whose officers' mess have asked me to send them a pretty young Girl for the night. It is a regular thing with them when they muster after a refit. They always enjoy one of my Girls on the night before sailing. And tomorrow, alas, they sail on the eight o'clock tide in the morning – so you will be put ashore betimes!'

Then, no doubt seeing the alarm in my eyes, she added with a kindly smile, 'Have no fear, my little treasure. It will all be done with the greatest decorum, one at a time and in privacy. You will be dined in style, and wined in style . . . and then bedded in style. And they will treat you like a Young Lady from first to last for the rules there are the same as the rules here. And you will find in Commander F. the most perfect gentleman. Believe me, he will tolerate no nonsense of that kind from any of them.'

'Them?' I echoed, not quite daring to ask how many, for I thought it might sound unprofessional.

'Seven,' she said. 'From the commander to the young ensigns. You are obliged to Pleasure each of them once, for which the fee is already fixed at twenty guineas. So they are to get a good innings each . . . but I know you well enough by now to be sure you will not hasten them on and give poor value. After that, if any wish a second helping – or a third or fourth – it is for you to fix the fee in your usual way, depending on their desires. But at six in the morning prompt, and whether you have fully Pleasur'd your Lover of the moment or not, you will go to the Commander and give him his final hour of glory. And then you may render him your bill and he will pay you at sight. No other coin changes hands. But he will explain the system to you. They are all lovely boys, young or old. I never yet had a Girl complain of her treatment there – nor of the fees she earned in so short a time. So – up the stairs to Bedfordshire and get what sleep you can!'

Oh, Sweet Fanny, at all this talk of bed and sleep my eyes droop and my pen grows weary. I shall send this now, or my messenger with the book and prints may overtake my promises. And I shall tell of my night aboard HMS D in my next, which I shall write this Sunday, not waiting for your reply.

Ever yours, sweet nymph,
Frances
Comtesse de C.

PS: I mean what I say about exploring Miss Laycock beyond your Hymen. I have a most wonderful First Lover in mind for you. He is a French Aristocrat of the utmost refinement. Not only will he reward you handsomely, he will also send you delirious with Pleasure and teach you the Ways of Love so thoroughly you will be a very Queen among Courtesans. And whether you decide to enter the Family Trade or not, the enrichment he could bring you is still vast. *I have particular reason to be sure of that*. But he will not look at you if you are no longer intact. So if the Desires aroused by my letters inflame you beyond endurance, come at once to France and all shall be arranged. Indeed, perhaps that would be best. Like me, you should not decide on the Old Game until you know it's worth the candle – though if it *is*, then the candle is the first thing you'll throw away!

Enough of this. You see how tired and skittish I get!

LETTER THREE

FROM MOUNT VENUS,
Sunday, 10th March, 1850

Sweet Fanny,

Here, then, is the tale that tiredness forced me to abandon last Wednesday ere I had even begun it for you. A kindly Commander F., whom I shall henceforth call Felix, for the very reason that that is *not* his true name – though it means Happiness, which is the true nature of our Encounter that night – dear Commander Felix met my phaeton at the dockyard gates and brought me through a maze of wharfs and craneways to the berth where his ship, HMS D lay tied. I might have been, in truth, the chaplain's daughter, for his conversation in all that way – although we were perfectly alone together and he could, as my paymaster for the night, have taken what liberties he liked with me – was of the most elevated kind.

'There she rides,' he said proudly as we drew up before the gangway.

To me she might as well have been a prison hulk. I don't imply that I felt imprisoned – not in the least – but all vessels above a certain size are one to me.

Still, I have known men take pride in the strangest of things, all connected with their authority and command, so I passed some suitable compliment on her appearance and bulk, and then we went aboard. Mrs Featherstone-haugh's coachman brought my bag, which held various items of clothing – hareem pantaloons, diaphanous blouses, and such like, which were then all the rage, and, of course, my Golden Douche which the Comte had given me. The bosun's piping as we stepped on deck took me completely by surprise, I may add. Commander Felix said 'twas in my honour, but I know that was just his kindly way. I think he sensed the trepidation within me, for this night's work would be something new and strange.

Part of me anticipated it keenly; I cannot deny that my own Sensual Pleasure has always been heightened by the element of compulsion or obligation that goes with the Trade. Perhaps it is the way I bury the last shreds of that guilt which I, as a vicar's daughter, must surely still feel in the unswept corners of my mind. If necessity obliges me to open my thighs to a Man, then there is nothing I can do or say to change the situation; then I have the simple choice of enduring it sullenly (but with an outward show of false passion, like a whore) or seeking my own Joy in the Union, like a true Lady of Pleasure; and since Bounteous Nature has brimmed me over with a capacity in that direction, it is the course I have chosen.

20

But part of me was also filled with anxiety, though of a remote and nebulous kind. I could not name it, and nor, I'm sure, could my charming Commander Felix, for all his experience in the situation; but he did his best to set me at my ease – and very largely succeeded, too. As soon as I arrived in the mess, we all sat down to dine. Not a second of the opportunity my presence offered them was to be wasted, though no one mentioned why, not even by a smirk or a wink.

They were as motley a crew as any average night in any regular House will serve a girl. Felix I have mentioned already; the others I will also name falsely. Henry, the surgeon, was a stocky, muscular little chap, shorter than me, but with a twinkle in his eye that promised fair. Jimmy One I didn't like the look of at all, a long, lank, surly man with a cold cast to his face and a gaze that could not meet me; I would have trouble with him, I felt, though of what sort I could not then say. Roderick was a family man and should never have been in the Navy at all; throughout the dinner he never once met my eye, though I had the impression it was from embarrassment rather than anything worse. I would have to do something special for Roderick, I decided – and how right I was, as you shall see! William was as solid as the Rock of Gibraltar. Of all the Men there he was the one most easily recognizable by any Gay Woman. He ate and drank with measured ease; he spoke sparingly and with manly assurance; and I suspected that when his time with me arrived, he would perform in the same smooth and reliable way. No fears there. Narcissus, one of the two young ensigns on board that night, was a giggler. He would gaze at me endlessly until our eyes met – and then he would look away at once and giggle at whatever anybody said, whether funny or not. Still, I thought, if I could settle him to it early, he'd not regret the extra item on his mess bill at the end of that month.

Adonis, the other young ensign, I have left till last, for that is when I meant to Enjoy him. And when I say *I* meant to Enjoy *him*, oh my sweet Fanny, I mean exactly that. He was a veritable young god, as fair as I was dark and as curly haired as I am straight; and with a body as trim and supple as any young girl might dream on – especially in that gorgeous uniform which even the youngest and most junior naval officer wears on full mess nights. Had I not been in the Fortunate Trade I was, I swear I should have paid him all that night's earnings just to enjoy his Favour once – and I hoped to Entice him to many more Passages of Arms than that!

So – there was my night's employment! And as the thought occurred to me, so, too, did the realization of what had made me uneasy as I prepared to board that ship.

Here we are, I thought, seven Lusty Men about to face months at sea, far from all Female company . . . seven men who, in the very nature of our meeting there, must already feel their Lust for my Young Body surging in their veins as they dream of the many ways they will roger me before the dawn . . . and here is sweet little me, wondering what those ways will be, and will I discover something new and marvellous (or will I be equal to them all?) . . . and while all that is passing through our minds, what are we actually *doing?* Why, talking and dining as decorously as if we were at a church Sunday Treat! It was a new situation to me, for though I had often Pleasur'd as many Men in an evening before, I had never seen them lined up beforehand like that. I tell you, Sweet Fanny, toward the end of that meal, as the incongruity of what we were at and what we would shortly be at grew more stark by the minute, it was all I could do to restrain my laughter.

And when Felix at last rose and said, 'Gentlemen, please enjoy the port in my absence,' I knew I had to say something, too.

22

He took me by the arm and led me to the door, for his room lay at the far end of the passage from the mess. As I rose, I took off my little bonnet and slipped out my combs and let my hair tumble down. It was a dramatic gesture for it reached, as I told you, to below my waist. The remaining officers gasped in unison and the moment was frozen on their sighing. Every eye there was rivetted upon me as I crossed the room at Felix's side – me being nearer the table. At the door, acting on the purest impulse, which came I know not whence, I turned and said, in the demurest, sweetest voice, 'Gentlemen! It would be absurd to leave you in silence, without once mentioning the cause of our joyous meeting here tonight. I thank you for what has already been a veritable feast, but I hope it is the merest portent of the feasting to come.' I glanced swiftly and in turn at each but my gaze lingered on Adonis; a Bargain of Pleasure was forged between us in that instant that had nothing to do with Trade or Obligation. It was the Ardent, Burning Desire of two young persons, prick'd to bursting by each other's Beauty. Be the other six as dull as dildos, I knew tonight would linger in my memory for ever.

And so I left them, half-ready to spend where they sat.

Felix, though he must have been a veteran at the Old Game, was shivering at my side. 'Minx!' he whispered admiringly as we reached his cabin door.

'Forgive me,' I said as I went in before him. 'I could not help it. All the way here I have been so excited – and now that I have met your gallant officers, I am at a fever pitch to exchange soft for hard and Enjoy them all.'

'Stop,' he laughed, stuffing his fingers in his ears. He meant he did not believe me and thought it all mere banter to ease those awkward first moments.

'Truly, my dear,' I assured him. 'Sweet young Miss Laycock and I have languished at the Academy this

23

month and more, yearning for the touch of a good Man. And all we have known is callow youths' – I held out my little finger, ramrod stiff but pathetic in size – 'and weakling landlubbers.' I held out my thumb, bent at the joint.

'Enough,' he murmured and pulled me gently into his embrace. I melted at the size and power of him. Young Adonis, I realized, should not get my All tonight.

He stroked my hair, all the way down to my *derrière*, where he lingered lovingly, and smelled my perfume, sighing at a passion he was now hard put (and I mean *hard*!) to contain. Adroitly he turned me round and cradled me into him, now running his hands up and down the front of me, feeling all my curves. I was filled with an enormous sense of confidence in his skills as a Lover and felt no unease at abandoning myself to him utterly. Some Ladies of Pleasure will save themselves to the last Lover of the night, fearing that if they spend themselves early they will burn out; but that was never my trouble – rather the other way about: If I spent early I would spend with all the rest, whether they were to my taste or not – for a Woman on that plateau does not descend so quick as a Man. 'Tell me what you Desire of me,' I whispered, covering his lips with soft, brief kisses, 'and I shall do it.'

'Oh! How shall I live at sea without this?' he asked in a voice made rough by his longing.

'By making the most of it now.'

'What I wish,' he went on, 'is to undress you slowly – to take off every stitch – while I stay in full uniform, you understand?'

I nodded – and shivered, for it has always been a foible of mine to be embraced by a man in full military uniform while I am naked as a babe.

'And then I shall discover you . . .' He spoke now like one possessed, unable to vary his actions or words in the slightest degree. 'With my eyes. With my fingers. With my hands. With my lips. With my tongue. Again – you understand? I want to explore every part of you.'

Once more I nodded. 'And then I shall do the same for you?'

He let out a deep sigh. 'You do! You do understand!'

After that there was little need for words. Despite our difference in years we were both seasoned in the action and I knew how to wriggle and twist my Body and hide and offer her Secrets so that he almost died of Joy. As, indeed, did I when his skilled and gentle fingers parted Miss Laycock's twin lips and his own closed around her rosebud to hide the suckling and grazing of his tongue. Oh, Sweet Fanny, I almost brim over again at the memory of it now! I certainly did then – and he saw it and was delighted.

'Now me,' he said. But he stayed my hand at the first button. 'Is there anything you wish of me before you do this?'

I blushed – I mean, I blushed even more than my first Ecstasy had induced me to. 'There is one thing I have never yet done,' I confessed.

'Ask it now.'

'May I take out your Ruffian and give him some air – for I'm sure he feels himself in prison there?'

He nodded and gave me a quizzical smile. I bent my nimble little fingers to his fly and soon had him free and easy. Those rods of gristle Men employ to our mutual Pleasure are as unique as their faces; I think I have never seen two identical. Dear Felix's was magnificent – neither too long nor too thick. (Men believe length and girth is highly exciting to us – little do they know how our hearts sink at the sight of the largest of them. I shall say more on this in a moment – and, if you take to the Trade, I'll tell you a dodge or two to avoid letting the

25

worst of them in.) Anyway, Felix was now lying on his back, in the full mess dress of a naval commander, and with his perfect ramrod free as air. I, naked to my toenails, then threw myself upon him and put my Nipples to his lips, offering him one and then the other, swiftly, by turns. I have told you how they harden and swell even when my Excitement is but meagre, so you may imagine the effect of this splendid exercise upon me! Then, when he had brought me back near my Ecstasy, I slid myself down over all his buttons and braid until John Thomas, who had lingered hot and throbbing between my knees (which had helped him along with many a gentle squeeze) now lay hard against Miss Laycock's trembling veils.

'Not into you yet,' he said in alarm.

'Indeed, no,' I agreed with all my heart – for I was as keen to prolong our Pleasure now as he.

And there, with scarcely a movement to provoke it – just hugging the dear bulk of him beneath me, and feeling his racing pulse in that lovely Engine at my vestibule, I brimmed over once again – which, as it began to flag, he helped sustain by raking his fingernails up and down my back and taking up my hair and tickling me with its ends.

And so, when that Spasm was done, I undressed him, clout by clout, folding each as carefully as he had folded mine – saying not a word, but with our eyes fastened in one long and happy smile. Then, when he lay as naked as me, and still on his back, I straddled him once more and discovered his Body with the same loving care he had used on me.

His Nipples (as is the case with some Men) were as erotically sensitive as mine. When I suckled on one and stroked the other, he pushed me sharply away – and then hugged me to him to show his brusqueness had been urgent rather than angry. 'When I tell you I want to spend,' he murmured, 'caress me there like this.' And he demonstrated on mine – which started me on my next cycle of Pleasure with him (and he noted it, too). 'Meanwhile . . . they are tiger country to you.'

I explored the rest of him and finally took his bone into my mouth – which I had for long minutes been provoking him into expecting. Do you find the very thought of it disquieting, Fanny dear? Then wait till my French lord has finished your schooling – you will think it as natural as allowing Miss Laycock to engulf him entire. But here, being uncertain of your response, and being unwilling in the extreme to provoke you to anything but Pleasure in my recollections, I shall pass over all further detail. Suffice it to say that I soon had him so hot he must enter me or burst.

Indeed, I had overdone my Stimulation, for no more than five minutes had passed (when I knew him capable of twenty or more) before he was throbbing away inside me and filling me with that warm, sensuous Milk from which we lucky Females derive so much of benefit to our skins and hair – while theirs, poor darlings, falls out at the continual outpouring of the same pearly Elixir! We had enjoyed no more than half a dozen Positions and I felt quite deflated, for there was so much more I thought we might Enjoy together. I spent a little with him but nothing like the overpowering Sensations I had so looked forward to.

'You will be back?' he said, half-command, half-request.

'Nothing could prevent me,' I promised him as I stepped swiftly back into my clothes. 'Who's next?'

He gave me a sympathetic grin. 'I should get Jimmy One over and done with, if I were you.'

I hesitated.

'He has no love of Women, poor chap, and yet he cannot leave them be. He'll roger you once and then wish you damned in Hell.'

You may imagine how my alarm increased at hearing this. 'We of Mrs Featherstonehaugh's Academy,' I pointed out, all businesslike again, 'do not offer Discipline – either in giving or receiving.'

'Oh, have no fear on that score. There are backsides enough already on board to satisfy him in that line. No, he is as enslaved by Woman as any man alive – but 'tis a slavery he cannot abide. He will not harm you, for he knows he would answer to me, but he will be cold and brusque.'

'Oh, I can manage that,' said I blithely – but *certes* I went with leaden feet.

I gave Jimmy One my most fetching smile, but all he said – cold and brusque as Felix had promised – was, 'Get naked, woman, and bend yourself over that chair. I want as little contact with you as possible so let's get it over and done with.'

I obeyed silently, putting at much Coquetry as I knew into my undressing for him. 'You may save that for the rest,' he said. 'To me you're just carrion.'

And this was a man who had paid three guineas for the Privilege! I tell you – their ways sometimes pass all comprehension!

I bent over the back of his chair, as directed, and slipped my fingers between my thighs to part Miss Laycock's lips and let him in. Under my arm I watched him take out his Pego, which was small and pale, and I felt I understood something of his difficulty. But imagine my surprise when instead of presenting himself at Miss Laycock's door he offered to break down Miss Brown's!

'Here!' I said at once, 'I'm having none of that.'

'You shall,' he answered stoutly. 'Else you'll get no pay from me.'

'So be it,' I answered, reaching for my clothes.

But as I did so, I caught such a look in his eye . . . such

a sad, haunted look, that it gave me pause. 'Is it really what you wish?' I asked in a more conciliatory tone.

'Aye!' He snapped back into his former coldness.

But I had glimpsed another man within him and some little She-devil within me began to wonder if he could not be reached. I fluttered my eyelashes at him and made my bosoms heave. 'You must understand I have never permitted such a thing before . . .'

That was a lie, of course, for the Comte and I had done everything – but *everything*; yet it was true I had never permitted it in the way of Trade before that night.

And his pego *was* enticingly small for that sort of work.

And I hate to relinquish a fee and send a Lover disgruntled away.

'Will it hurt?' I asked, allowing my voice to shiver.

The notion excited him and I knew I could drive him up above three guineas.

'Shouldn't think so,' he said. 'Isn't it a whore's stock-in-trade?'

'But I am not a whore,' I told him. 'I am a Lady of Pleasure. Suppose we tried it?' I bit my lip uncertainly. 'Would you be gentle with me to start with?'

'Aye,' he gulped. His blood was racing now despite his would-be coldness.

'And withdraw at once if I said it hurt?'

'Aye, aye – of course!' I could see the pulse that hammered at his throat.

'But I could not permit it for three guineas,' I went on sadly. 'It is, after all, the loss of a kind of virginity – and that is always rewarded extra.'

'Double,' he said eagerly. 'I'll pay you double.' And to my surprise he snatched up a chit of paper and wrote on it 'IOU Three guineas,' and signed it with a hasty scrawl.

'What use is this to me?' I asked as he pressed it into my hand. 'With you at sea before noon tomorrow?'

29

He was equally baffled. 'Did our gallant Commander not explain the system to you then?'

I shook my head.

'Every service you perform over and above the first round, you'll agree the fee with the officer concerned and he'll give you his IOU – which the Commander will redeem in gold before you leave.'

I took it then and bent myself over the chair again. 'Remember now,' I said. 'Be gentle. And . . .'

He once again butted his pego importunately against Miss Brown.

'No, no!' I cried. 'Put your fingers down *there* first and take up some of my own juices. Spread them gently round my Entrance and on your Mighty Engine. Then it will go easier for us both.'

He was as rough about it as you might expect. 'Easy!' I cried once again – yet with a little laugh, too. 'Pretend she is a little furry mouse who would be crushed by such manly handling.'

Humour worked where nothing else would or could. He was suddenly as gentle with me as I could wish. And I think he was as surprised as I for now he lingered at his work of lubricating Miss Brown with my juice.

'Here,' I said, my voice deep and slightly breathless, 'that's not at all unpleasant, you know.'

It was not my idea of pleasant, either, mind but at least I knew it was not going to hurt. Pain is one thing I cannot stand.

'May I?' I asked in that same soft tone, and, without waiting for an answer, I took up some moisture of my own, and bending even lower to reach my hand through my legs, began to massage the half-exposed knob of him. He shivered with Desire. 'Come on, then,' I said, giving it a light tug. 'Gently does it. Show your little girlie what she's been missing all this time.'

Now he did not trust himself to speak. Slowly he obeyed my urging and pushed himself against Miss Brown once more. This time there was no resistance from me. 'In,' I urged impatiently. 'Slowly in.'

As soon as I felt the knob of him inside, I gave out a little cry of Joy – as if the very surprise of it had almost brought me close to spending.

'You needn't fake for me,' he said – brusque still but with a hint of kindliness there, as if he were letting me off some unpleasant duty.

'Feel my Nipples if you think I feign my Delight,' I told him.

And they, little darlings, bore me out as usual.

After that he was almost pleasant with me. And I don't know why it is but when a Man has been harsh with us and then has relented – even into mere civility – we are somehow more taken with him than with a Man who was civil from the start. And so I found it now with Jimmy One. I did not spend with him, nor even come near my Ecstasy, and yet I cannot deny I took a certain minor pleasure in the feel of his little pego rogering away in the wrong place.

'You may thrust a little harder if you will,' I pleaded with breathless abandon when I felt him rising to his climax there. He was quick to comply and, as I had hoped, it made him spend at once – and copiously. I squeezed to his timing with those muscles we can use at will, and cried out my own feigned Delight in time with his. I'm sure the whole mess heard us.

As I left him I turned and said, 'If you want me to come back to you later tonight, I could teach you other forms of Pleasure, even greater than that.'

He used a number of coarse terms to the effect that he did not wish to bathe his pego in the milt of his brothers. 'Even without that,' I promised him.

31

He nodded curtly. 'Very well.' A ghost of a smile lingered on his lips but he exorcised it smartly.

No matter. I had seen it. And I had seen, too, the eagerness with which he had signed away an extra three guineas. He was not short of gold.

Henry was next, my strong and stocky surgeon. He knew exactly what he Desired of me, undress'd me efficaciously, disposed my unclothed Body in several Lascivious Positions and enjoyed me mightily in each. If all our Lovers were such as he, with just one Felix or one Adonis added for our own Delectation each day, then girls like you, Sweet Fanny, would need no such urging as mine to enlist in our Regiment.

My remaining four Lovers doubled up in a couple of cabins that were, in any case, too small for the Pleasures of Venery to have free scope. The dining room had therefore been transformed, with a sprinkling of cushions and straw palliasses, into a snug Temple of Love, where I was now installed as Goddess and my Devotees came to me. There were also candles and mirrors and a wash basin – all the usual appurtenances.

I made one or two small adjustments, tried out the chairs and table for height and position, and so on, and then sent for Roderick. The poor dear was all a sweat and a tremble – but not, as I saw it once, from Craving after me. 'Twas fear, unalloyed. I made my usual preliminary remarks but he seemed not to hear. 'You will not tell the others?' he blurted out at last.

'Tell them what, pray?' I asked.

'About me. That I . . . you know.'

'That you would rather sit and talk for a wee while?' I suggested.

He nodded miserably.

Since I would not, for the next four Bouts, be moving up and down the corridor, I decided to slip into my other

clothing – the diaphanous blouse and the hareem pantaloons. A good show I gave him of my changing, teasing
him with 'artless' Revelations of my Charms. I could see
his interest shining in his eyes; he was not one of those who
prefer young boys to us Women. But it led to no Action on
his part. During this time I also used my Golden Douche,
which is of a solution of Jesuit Bark, a highly efficacious
barrier to would-be little babies. In fact, Sweet Fanny,
now that I am upon this matter (and since my poor
Roderick is more 'ick' than 'rod'!) let me dispel your fears.

You asked how a Lady of Pleasure can avoid 'breaking
her ankle', as the saying goes, when she has the milt of so
many Lovers poured into her each day. In truth, I think
that is the very trick of it. See what happens when the
boys of one school accidentally meet those of another,
when the youth of one street go *en masse* among that of
one nearby, when the lads who support this prizefighter
meet them who fancy another – why, 'tis up fists and
black eyes and broken lips and spitting blood in triumph
all the way home. And no matter what their original
object may have been, their fighting claims precedence
over all. I believe 'tis precisely the same when the milt
of one man meets that of another inside. The little
homunculi, or whatever they pass to quicken us, fall out
among themselves and kill each other off. At all events, I
can assure you there is no epidemic of new feet for baby
boots in our Houses of Pleasure up and down the land. I
use my Golden Douche very much in the spirit of that
cautious duke who, going to Ascot, always had a second,
empty carriage follow him a mile after.

The astringency of the Jesuit Bark has the effect of
removing my own juices for a while, so there I employ
another little Dodge of the Comte's – namely some tiny
lozenges of calf's-foot jelly in which, for good measure,
there is also cocoa butter and a little more essence of

33

Jesuit Bark. This restores all my natural Lubrication and leaves me eager for the Lucubration of my next Lubricious Lover.

So here I am, back with poor Roderick, his Spirit all willing, his Flesh all weak. As he is in his nightshirt, I lay us down side by side, me naked, and I cradle him in my arms, lying a little upon me with his head between my breasts. And I begin to tell a Salacious Tale of my first Experience with a Lover at the age of nine. 'Twas all invented, of course, if taken as the truth concerning me; and yet 'twas all true, for I knew the girl that told it me. Perhaps I shall tell you at some later time, as the occasion arises, for 'tis quite instructive and gives the lie to those who would have us believe little girls are all sweet and pure young Innocents.

I chose this tale because I suspected the poor man felt in some strange manner cowed and threatened by my too easily available Femininity. The sight of a Voluptuous Young Woman naked and at close quarters, the Heat of her Body, the Aroma of her Sex, the Roguish Challenge of her eyes . . . these are powerful Stimulants to any Man. No wonder that in some it can overload his Desire and break its back. I have seen sturdy Young Bucks in the drawing room below reduced to a shivering mass when it is skin to skin, and it has taken some smart work on my part, I may tell you, to mend their Lust before the change was irreversible. Thus my tale of little me and my own little Miss Laycock, bald as a baby and too small to take a pencil lead, bringing off an ageing Satyr by friction alone and crying tears of terror and Joy at my own first Ecstasy . . . all this was designed to put him at ease.

I had no greater hope of him during that first lying-together, but I knew that, for his Honour's sake alone, he would sign his IOU for a further bout, and I supposed I might manage something with him then.

He listened in rapt silence and then gave out a great sigh – just as if he had spent himself utterly. The sound of it must have awakened him to his true situation for he made an embarrassed little cough and begged me utter the cries he had heard me give out with Jimmy One.

'But I cannot do that without help,' I teased.

He was all dismay again. 'But I . . . I mean . . . you know how it is with me.'

'You have fingers,' I reminded him. 'And see here. 'Tis time to feed my Dumb Glutton one or two of my special little lozenges. You may do it for me.'

He was almost hesitant and gingerly about it. 'You may work a little harder than that,' I assured him. 'I am no longer nine, you know.'

He was no stranger to a Woman's Secret Places, for he knew all the strokes and touches that set our blood a-racing – better than most Men, indeed, who, without instruction, are lamentable at that Art. I suspected that was the only form of Pleasure he had been able to give his wife these years past, and that she had taught him it. Truth to tell, he did manage to rouse me a little and, as the lozenge dissolved and its juice replenished my own, I found it easy to give out those cries of Joy he so desired to hear.

'What is in those pills?' he asked in wonder when I had done. He sniffed his fingers and then licked them. 'Cocoa?' he asked, more mystified than ever.

I winked. 'My own Trade secret. I make them up myself after a receipt given me by a French Lover I once knew – a man most adept in all the Arts of Venus.'

'But what does it do?'

'Isn't it obvious? Did you not observe? When on nights like this my Desire begins to wane – out of surfeit of Stimulation, you follow – my little Lozenges restore it to a fever pitch. Indeed' – I rose from our bed and slipped into my flimsy attire – 'send me William as fast as he'll come. I am faint with it already.'

But he did not move. 'Do they . . . ah, work on me, too?' he asked.

'They do.' I told him as if I had forgot. In truth, this twist to my lie had only then occurred to me. 'Taken by mouth they act more slowly, of course.' I offered him the box. 'Have two – go on, do. And when you hear me slip in to Jimmy One for his second . . .'

'Him?' He stared at me incredulously. 'He's given you his chit for *another* go?'

I showed it him. 'Then I think you are a very Witch of Venery,' he murmured admiringly. And he gave me his chit, too.

At the sight of William my heart, indeed, fell into my boots. *He* stood in the doorway, in his nightshirt, grinning like an ape. He stood at the threshold but the tip of his Yard (and I choose the word with care) was already half way across the room, bearing out his shirt before him like a spinnaker. 'Now there's a ruffian to stir the belly of a sweet young girl!' he told me admiringly.

'Oh!' I cried with every sign of delight – in which was mingled an all too genuine dismay. And I fell to my knees before It and, taking It in my hands – gathering the material around It by so doing – began to kiss It fervently as if It were a long-lost pet.

He pulled away hastily and I guessed he had a shaven trigger, as we say. 'Time enough for that,' he cried. 'For the moment all I want is a quick scrape. Get off the barnacles and rake out the curds. Just slip out of those pantaloons and we'll thrash away at once.'

'Oh, please,' I begged, slipping my hand under his shirt. 'It is not often I see so magnificent a tool as this. Wait till I tell the other girls! We all fought for the privilege of this night beneath you splendid men. Do let me adore It a little – and get used to the idea of It, too?'

'Well . . . very well,' he said, flattered into relenting. He took his shirt and stood there for my worship.

I had my hand about It now, half-way down and in a place of no danger. Fortunately It was of normal girth. The worst is when they are as thick as your wrist as well as long. This one, I swear, was full eleven inches from thrusting bone to knob. If I let him ram away to the hilt, as no doubt he wished with me, he would leave me ruined for the night.

'May I . . . kiss it?' I asked shyly.

'Only along the top,' he warned. 'Else you might spend me in the air. By God but he's ready for a Bit of Snug. Three strokes and he'll spout like a whale.'

I could not have picked a better simile myself, I thought as I lowered my lips to Its pale, throbbing skin. As you will be shown, Sweet Fanny, if you follow my scheme for you, the flesh all along the skyward half of a man's Bowsprit (in the standing Position), is no more susceptible to Erotic Stimulus than, for instance, the skin of his palm – that is to say, but slightly. All his Excitable Cravings are gathered in the lower part of his Knob (the bit which always reminds me of a fish's gills when seen from below) and in the duct or conduit that forms Its spine (if you suppose It to be lying on Its back, that is). The reason for this I have already half told you. The skin of Miss Laycock's throat is rough on the half near Miss Fawcett and smooth on the half near Miss Brown. Randy Mother Nature has designed us, Men and Women, to Enjoy each other *à la doggy*, for that brings the rough throat into Delicious Friction with the most Excitable parts of Old Polyphemus, the one-eyed monster.

The point of this is, if you have some urgent reason to bring a man off swiftly, make like a gazelle and offer him yourself *a verso* – not, I hasten to add, for him to enjoy

37

Miss Brown (unless that be your bargain with the Man), but to yield Miss Laycock at her most Thrilling to him. And there was my dilemma. I did, indeed, have most urgent reason to bring my William off as swift as maybe, but I could not possibly offer that vast length of him my *derrière*.

'I cannot kiss Him properly with you standing like that,' I told him. 'Lie down, do.'

Delighted at my adoration, he complied willingly. At once I straddled him – not, as you might imagine, in the usual way, head-to-head, feet-to-feet. He would have been fly enough to have seen through that. Instead I knelt over him, thighs wide apart and sweet Miss Laycock gazing down upon him with her beauteous vertical grin. He could not resist Her *open* invitation, of course, and began at once to play with Her frills and folds, working my Juices all over Her lips; and I, for my part, bent to my work and took Him into my mouth. In this Alignment, as you will readily understand from what I have explained, there is little risk of bringing a Man off, for your tongue, who is a marvellous little *fricatrice*, cannot work on the side where his Craving is.

My thought was, you see, that if I could give him as much Thrill outside me as possible, I should earn my fee and he have no complaint. I worked away in this fashion, fondling his snails and gently scratching the inside of his thighs from time to time, until I felt him begin to weary. Then, with a sigh of utmost Pleasure, I lowered Miss Laycock to his lips and let him feast his fill. In this Position we saw off several minutes more. I let my breathing grow wilder and more disordered – though, in truth, I was so fearsome of this Mighty Yard I felt no Thrill of my own at all; even my Nipples remained soft as marshmallows.

Then, when I had made it seem I was on the verge of

38

spending, I flung myself round and, straddling him, thrust Miss Laycock down over Him and took Him as far into Paradise as seemed comfortable to me. He was too surprised to protest; and his rashness did the rest. I have particular muscles down there, which are not found, or not capable of exercise, in many other Women. They are not quite the same as those that choke off Misses Fawcett and Brown; they lie – as you would expect – somewhere in between. And they do not so much choke off Miss Laycock as cause her to squeeze Old Hornington as a milkmaid's hand draws milk from an udder. I believe they do so spontaneously when I am in a true Erotic Delirium with a Lover but I am then too far gone to know or care; however, I have found them useful with that majority of Lovers who rouse me to but mild Pleasure (if that) – and so I employed them now, crying out the while as if *in extremis veneris*.

He was right about his own short fuse. A second later he was spending what must have been a week of continence up into me – and Miss Laycock gulping it down as if she had passed that same week in *Arabia Deserta* (whereas, to pursue the metaphor, she had passed each night in Storm and Deluge!). When I am not particularly Moved by a Lover, I sometimes content myself by counting the number of Throbs to his entire Thrill; each Throb, you know, is the Gift to us of one more packet of milt – generous at the start, niggardly toward the finish. Again the variation among Men is amazing. One, who Lov'd me dearly for many years, never made but two Throbs or three and then fell fast asleep; only for half a minute or so – but sound and genuine slumber. The most I ever counted in any Man was forty-one; and then, when I moved to get him off me, thinking he had steeped it long enough for his fee, he said no, there was more. Maybe there were, but too faint for me to share.

I let my William steep It as long as he wished, lying side by side now, deliciously entwin'd. When he pulled It out I was astonished to see It shrivelled to no more than an ordinary size. 'You did that,' he commented lugubriously.

'He'll be back in an hour,' I promised in a husky whisper that I have always found very effective.

I left my thighs parted wide for his Delectation, feeling I had not truly earned my fee even now. He saw his gravy on me where its surfeit had spilled out, and he took up his shirt to wipe it away. But I stayed him. 'Rub it gently in,' I begged, 'as it were an ointment or salve – which it is, indeed, you know.'

That gave him another few minutes for his fee. Our eyes held each other's and I felt very Warm towards him, though in no way Passionate for our next embrace. 'You are amazing ,' he told me – and truly meant it, I believe. 'You give so much to each. I have heard you through the walls here tonight. How do you keep it up?'

I laughed. 'It is not *I* who must keep it up, dear Bill!'

He laughed, too, but was not to be swayed from his point. 'You cannot be as Passionate with one as with all – if, in fact, you can be truly Passionate with any.'

'But I love Men,' I assured him. 'All kinds and conditions of men, young and old, tall and short, fat and thin . . .'

'And do you really believe this spunk has any powers as a salve? Surely you cannot? This is just for my Pleasure. Be honest now.'

Never, Sweet Fanny, accede to that command, however tempting it may be!

Gently I raised my fingers to my face. Perhaps the idea had already formed in my mind – how to keep It at bay next time round. The just shaping of a Passage of Arms between a Lady of Pleasure and her Lover is like unto the making of a poem or painting, I often feel: the impulse that directs it and gives it such pleasing Form comes we known not whence; yet we can all recognize its Majesty when the deed is done. 'How,' I murmured in a voice filled with invitation, and running the tips of my fingers gently over my cheeks and brow, 'how do you suppose I am so free of spots and blemishes here – which are ever the plague of Young Girls who see little of the sun and too much of the moon?'

The notion at once took root in him. I saw a sudden glint in his eye. I heard his hesitation at a promise I had made and yet not quite made. 'You mean . . .?' he asked, caressing my cheeks with the back of his dry hand.

I nodded solemnly and let my eyes go dark and wide.

'Then you would not mind . . .' He gulped and burst out with: 'God, I have so often pictured it, during long months at seas, yet never actually . . .' He licked his lips and breathed in courage. 'You mean you would not mind my old Spermspouter here, squirting away all over this beautiful face . . . these matchless features?'

I lowered my eyes and said, as if in deepest reluctance, 'You must not be swayed by any Desires of mine. You must feel free to have your way with me – whatever is your wish.'

His yard was climbing skyward at the very thought; it was amazing to see it grow. He signed me his IOU, making it for six guineas without my prompting, guessing that to be the fee for something so special as he next intended. And I was pleased enough not to have him wrecking my belly at our next Encounter I would have played Pan's Pipes for free.

Poor Narcissus! The very friction of drawing up his shirt as he stood before me fetched him off at once. I grabbed him swiftly and squeezed as Miss Laycock would have done had she been given the chance; and the little pearly blobs of his milt raced through the air between us and plastered the skin of my belly. All the while he giggled like something in the zoo. I hastily thrust down my pantaloons with my free hand and massaged it in as it came. I did not jest when I told William it was a salve, for I truly believe it to be the most efficacious unguent a Woman can put upon her skin, and we Ladies of Pleasure are the most fortunate Women alive who have so ready and copious a supply of it.

To be sure, you must sponge it off within half an hour or you will soon reek of the gluepot; but by then it has done its magic.

Narcissus, who still had not stopped his inane giggling, gave me his IOU for a further three guineas but I made him change it to one, since I could not charge more for so brief an Encounter and told him he could do whatever he pleased next time, when he would be less importunate.

And so at last, sponging myself pure again, and combing my hair, and refreshing the traces of that subtle perfume my darling Comte had devised especially for me and which I had sent from Paris each month . . . at last I opened my arms – and every other part of me – to my darling Adonis! Yet (and I hope I do not disappoint you in this – though I fear I shall) I feel I have less to record of our Encounter than with any other Officer that night, save perhaps Narcissus.

The truth is that when I give my Self, my whole, entire Self, my every nerve and heartbeat to my Lover (and whether he pays or not is immaterial here) and he gives his Self in like vein to me, I cannot afterward remember *what* we did! I know I began to Thrill, in that minor way which is possible to a Woman but not, it seems, to a Man, the moment he crossed the threshold; and thereafter 'tis all clouds of dreams and gaspings and delirium and all manner of sweetness and Love. The moment our Bodies were joined – and I cannot tell whether that was a minute

42

or an hour after we began – we were as one Carnal Being, one Flesh at Riot and Disorder. I am sure I fainted at least once at the sheer overwhelming voluptuousness of our Union.

And when it was done we fell at once into the profoundest slumber, still notched, and him still hard.

Half an hour later that iron-souled gaoller Conscience brought me wide awake. My Adonis had gone and where his sweet head had laid was a simple note: 'We should never better that, my darling Fanny, not if we tried all night. I give you my chit for three guineas more. Had I a thousand times as much, you should have that, too. But I pray you do not send for me when you do your rounds again; I want to remember you at your dearest and most precious best this next long year at sea. Yet assure yourself of this: The moment we are docked again upon these shores, no matter where, the Bee with the Sting will make his line directly to your Honeypot and there feast himself a night and a day.'

I never saw him again, dear granddaughter. Men are like that. But I never let myself fret. There are plenty more like him in that vast sea of Man-flesh, and we who trawl so wide can always find one or two in our nets.

Also, to be candid, I did not mind his refusing me another Bout. He was right – it could not have been half so good. But at even a quarter so good he would still have left me unsettled for the work that still lay ahead of me. I went at once to my dear Felix, who soon put me back in more Professional mood.

But 'tis past four here at Château C. and even the owls have done their courtship by now, so the rest of that night must wait another day and another epistle than this. Do not fret that you put me to such labours; I cannot tell you what Joy it has given me to recall that particular night. However, I am aware that my Enjoyment is not to the purpose in all this. I also have a particular reason – something for your Instruction – for reviving these particular memories when I have a thousand others among which to choose. But it must wait till my next – which I promise will be soon.

Ever yours, sweet nymph,
Frances
Comtesse de C.

LETTER FOUR

MOUNT VENUS,
Wednesday, 13th March, 1850

Sweet Fanny,

I shall answer your most recent letter in a moment; it contains one grievous misunderstanding, which, fortunately, is easily put right. But all in its proper place. Let me deal swiftly with the remainder of my night aboard HMS D. and draw your Instruction from it all.

My appointed Lovers for that night were, you will remember, seven in all. Five had rogered me in various ways, one had spent importunately into my hand, and one had achieved nothing – indeed, he had not even tried.

I was glad indeed that my second round began with

dear Felix rather than one of the others. He was ready for me this time and, having some of his Urgency blunted by our first Union, was more languorous and skilled with me. If Adonis was a sweet, sharp Pleasure, this new encounter with Felix was warm and profound. When a Lively Young Girl has her Body used by an adept and kindly Man, no matter what their difference in years, there is an exquisite Pleasure in the very assurance of his handling. And I mean *hand*ling, for Felix's hands were always there where my Flesh craved most their gentle touch – now lifting me up to him, now clasping my hips . . . cupping my breasts, moving my willing young *derrière* this way and that to increase his Joy. And I was happy to become a mere toy – a 'lay figure' as painters call it – to be placed in this Position or that and so taken by him, from before, from behind, or ambushed from my flank.

That moment when my Holey of Holeys is first stretched by a Man's *arbor vitae* is always more exquisite to me than his second Thrust . . . and the second more sweet than the third . . . and so on. As salt can never lose its savour, so that primal expansion can never shed its slight surprise. And Felix seemed to know it, for now he withdrew himself entirely between each Thrust, making every Entry the most Thrilling of all; he enjoyed it for the contrast between the cool of the air on his wet skin and the warmth of my honepot all about him; for my part I gave back my encouragement in little sighs of joy and did my Special Squeeze as often as I could. I do not suppose there is one Position in the Lover's Lexicon we did not try that night. I thought my Adonis had drained me of my finest Ecstasy but Felix took me back up onto that Summit by such small and effortless steps I almost fell off the precipice when we both, at last, arrived.

And here you see the superiority of Women over Men.

We were both absolutely bathed in our own perspiration by the time he had fallen limp within me, and our hearts were pounding twenty to the dozen. His sweat had a marvellous, salty, bullish tang; mine (he swore) was sweet and dry like the finest hock! We just lay there and let it mingle awhile. He, being exhausted beyond measuring, just slumped upon me, but I, being younger, I suppose – and a Woman, too – was ready for more. I rolled him over and lay upon him and wriggled myself up and down, perfectly lubricated as if we had soaped each other all over; and I let my rosebud kiss the limpness that was all he could offer. And in that way I enjoyed two or three more Petty Thrills on my way back down the mountain.

And so I passed on once again to Jimmy One, whom I now taught to find a Passage of his own between my Breasts – with the help of certain oils which I always carry on my Visits of Charity. One of them has a slight tincture of wintergreen, which is to a man's Horn as is curry to the throat. Do not, however, allow it near Miss Laycock or Miss Brown, for their fine Flesh is more tender than a Man's and 'tis as if biting on a kar-de-mum within a curry to us. But it Thrilled him stupendously and he gave me an extra chit for five more guineas for my work. My Breasts being on the small side, they were perfectly suited to him.

Knowing he was utterly spent, in every way, by these Frolics, I coyly offered him another Go at Miss Brown, saying I had found it much more enjoyable that I would ever have imagined. To my dismay, however, I heard him say I had Pleasur'd him so mightily he would, when next ashore, come direct to Mrs Featherstonehaugh's Academy and renew our Joys. Unlike Adonis it was a promise kept. A year almost to the day he was back with his sweet little pego (and so I could think of it now, for he was almost warm with me) to renew his acquaintance with Miss Brown; and then, after bathing and powdering and a dish of tea and some pleasurable talk, he would go betwixt my Breasts as well – two Memorial Services in one! And he never paid under ten guineas for those Favours, either! So my efforts at a little kindly understanding were not wasted. By then, too, I would permit any Lover with a small or moderate pego to find his Pleasure with Miss Brown, if such were his bent; for, to tell the truth, they do not hurt at all at that size, and if the Lover himself is Adept with his fingers at my Rosebud and Nipples, the Pleasure is almost more Exquisite than usual. I never enjoyed a Mighty Ecstasy in that manner, but I had many a Minor Thrill.

William, to take him out of turn, I satisfied in like manner – between my Breasts, that is. His great Yard was not only long but banana-curved, so that when the hilt of him was between my Breasts, his Knob was in my mouth. That slowed his action down as he lingered there; but it raised the quality of his Pleasure beyond all reckoning. He, too, had never Experienced anything like it before, and the oil of wintergreen was so hot and rapturous he almost had an apoplexy when he spent, which he did as I had promised he might.

Roderick, who had swallowed my two lozenges the moment he heard me and Jimmy One cry out, was a picture of woe. Nothing had happened, he said lugubriously. But I gave him my confident smile. And, indeed, I now recalled I had Experience of this Malady before, at the Other White's Club (about which I must remember to tell you anon) and there I had made a small error, which I was determined not to repeat here.

I bade him lie down, which he did; and then I straddled him and bent forward until my lips were at his ear, pulling a blanket up over us at the same time so that he would feel as private as possible with me there. Then, in short little whisperings, pausing often to give his ears and neck the daintiest little Bites of Love, and to shower him with the most fleeting of Kisses, I reminded him of that sweet little nymph of nine (supposedly myself, you remember) who had been so frighted and so overjoy'd at her first true Ecstasy that her little heart almost leaped up her throat – and yet her Lover, that hoary, knowing old Satyr, had not even Penetrated her hymeneal gate.

I could feel *his* heart pounding away between my Breasts. I raised myself a little off him and put the edges of my thumbs to his tiny Nipples, wondering if he were one of those men who store their sensual electricity there. He was! I was sure of it the moment I touched him. He gave out a small cry of alarm – and of delight, commingled; but I smothered it with more whisperings, even as my thumbs began their slow, Sensual Magic. I assured him that Sweet Nymph was not dead. Indeed, she was there, hovering over him, buried within me and awaiting his call . . . it was all nonsense, to be sure, and yet it pacified him and – Miracle of Miracles! – Miss Laycock, smiling down on the field of our Engagement (if Engagement there would be), soon felt the weak and feeble knock of some half-firm Gristle.

He was beside himself with delight and wished to stuff It in at once – where It would surely have died in equally short order. But I was as firm with him in spirit as I wished to make him in the flesh. I continued exactly as before, caressing him and whispering suggestive nonsense in his ear. And ere long he was as Hot and Stiff as we could wish.

Then, indeed, I let him in and wriggled my belly upon him and indulged him with my Special Squeeze. After a goodly innings, when he almost fainted with forgotten Pleasures, he died within me and without spending; but I

49

had half-expected that. It did not matter, he chortled in his Joy. The Thing had returned to him. Oh, what Pleasure he could give his wife now! Or when next ashore.

And that was where I recalled my little error the last time this had happened. I revived that same 'Thing' for poor old Lord R–rry, who went all Hot and Lusty to his wife – only to find It shrivel as of old. 'Twas not established firm enough, you see.

'Please do no such thing,' I entreated him. 'You should know that few indeed are the Men who can remain powerless with a skilled Lady of Pleasure. This signifies nothing except that the flesh is not utterly dead. You may think this mere self-serving Cant – and I could not blame you if you do, for I know how mean and grasping many of my Sisters are. But as you love your Wife and Desire to Serve her truly, come back to me at the Academy when you are next ashore. I shall not have forgotten you, I promise – for this Revival has given me as much pleasure as it has you. And together we shall consolidate our small and perhaps passing Victory until it is *firm* enough to offer her whom you truly love.'

There were tears of gratitude in his eyes as he pressed upon me a further chit for five guineas.

Narcissus was a sweet little boy now his Urgency had gone. I gave him an Enormous Pleasure, for when a Man spends into the air he spends but a portion of what he has and there was plenty left for our second bout. Also, indeed, for a third, which took place between us 'toward two bells of the dog watch', or some such rigmarole. How curious that, of all my Lovers there that night, giggling little Narcissus should be the only man among them with three shots in his locker! But then I was once rogered for a dare, sixteen times in one night by a boy of fourteen, so, truly, quantity signifies nothing. The quality of the thing

50

is all. And of quality I believe I had given them plenty, don't you?

Henry! I forgot Henry, my stocky surgeon. Well, he was just the same the second time as the first. Knew what he wanted, put me in various Positions, and thrashed away with huge Delight. Nothing more to say.

At six, as arranged, I crept back into dear Felix's bed. But all he did was cradle me in his arms and fondle me delicately, even in the most private places, without once arousing either of us. And for the most part we talked of matters far removed from our Business of that night: of England and the beauties of her countryside that were being swallowed up by the Molochs of Industry; of Parliament and the Navy and the need for Reform (I swear it!); of Beethoven and Mozart; of greengages and the making of plum jam . . . and, oh, I know not what else – whatever came into our heads. And he was not fifty nor I twenty but we were two people who had enjoyed the sweetest Intercourse and now wished to lave it with the milk of ordinary humanity. And I truly think, my dear grandchild, that was the most delightful Bout of all, when we did nothing but talk – and learned how little divided us from each other.

Ah me – I even weep a little as I recall it now. I went back to dear Felix's ships five more times in all for those special eve-of-departure Orgies – until a storm carried him off and he was lost with all hands. And he called upon me more often than that during his leaves, at Mrs Featherstonehaugh's or wherever I was then working; and our Eager Bodies always made the sweetest music together. Dear Men – I loved them all in their different ways, and where are they now?

No, no – this will not do at all. This is not to my purpose here.

The Academy phaeton called for me at the appointed

51

hour and I was, indeed, piped ashore – in honour of a night of Perfect Engagements. And as I drove away I looked back at that great ship, which no longer had the faintest resemblance to a prison hulk, and I thought to myself – this night just passed has been a perfect Microcosm of my life as a Lady of Pleasure. There they go, all seven of my gallant Lovers, whom I had not met this time last night and who now know all my most Intimate and Thrilling Parts, as I do theirs . . . whom I may never meet again . . . and they had rogered me a dozen times between them, some to my unfathomable pleasure, most to my indifference, one (at first) to my alarm and discomfort . . . and I had handled three 'difficult customers' well, all to our mutual benefit . . . and I was tired but not sore . . . and I had been given more than my usual share of precious milt (for those crafty men had saved themselves up for me) . . . but above all, I had some fifty guineas by way of compensation.

And *that*, Sweet Fanny, is my answer to your original request to be told the tale of *one* Encounter with *one* Gentleman that would stand for the whole Way of Life. Do you see now why it would have been impossible?

Well, I have spared you nothing of the true nature of the Trade. I suppose you were not so foolish as to imagine a Lady of Pleasure's every Lover would be an Adonis; but it is easy for a foolish whore to turn them all – even the Adonises – into Jimmy Ones (as he was before I worked on him). So I trust you understand now a little more of the distinction I make between a whore (which I shall never be) and a Lady of Pleasure, which I have been from the moment I met the Comte until today – and God willing shall so continue.

Nor is that initial date an accident. The Comte it was who taught me all I ever knew; what else I may have learned is a mere palimpsest upon his sturdy foundation. I cannot overstress the importance of this. I, having run away as I did – after being caught by the verger with my hand in the curate's trousers (behind the altar of the Lady Chapel, of all places) and his milt all up my sleeve – would have taken to the streets anyway. But I should have been a sick, vindictive whore, hating men, and clapping them with rapture at every turn. The difference was this: *I met the Comte!*

Now here is where I must disabuse you of that error. Of course I do not intend that your first teacher should be that very same Comte! He is my *husband*, by all that's holy! More than that, he is your true grandfather . . . My mind quails that you could even suppose I *might* have meant such a thing.

Besides, he is over eighty now and his heart would not stand it; you are far too pretty and vivacious and young (and I think I may now add – eager, too?). But I have someone very close to him in mind, as you shall shortly learn. And I *know* he can do for you all that the Comte did for me. First let me tell you what that was.

There I stood, a rural vicar's daughter of fifteen, utterly ignorant of the world and its wiles – though wild mares could not have dragged such an admission from me then – freshly off the coach at the New Inn Yard in Cheapside and wondering what on earth to do next. You have the scene in *Fanny Hill*, indeed, and believe me, 'tis no fiction. Tens of thousands of young girls 'up from the country' to seek their fortune are taught in that same old manner they have been sitting on it fourteen or fifteen long years. The same kindly old woman had just taken up with me when my eye caught that of the Comte. You have heard of love at first sight? This was trust at first glance. I suddenly knew there was no one else in all the world I would trust but that man.

53

How? you may ask. I cannot answer you. All I know is that 'twas so from the instant our eyes met – he being then in the act of boarding his own private coach for Dover. He descended at once and threaded his way through the crowd towards me; I no longer heard what the kindly old woman was trying to tell me. I simply drifted away from her and towards him; we were as two magnets to each other – unlike poles that attract, I mean. A young girl of near sixteen and an aristocrat in the prime of his forties!

He took both my hands in his, very gently, applying no pressure – a thing he has never done. 'You have nowhere to go?' he asked. His English was better then than it is now, he having spent so many years in our country, and so few since.

'No,' I said, though suddenly I did not feel in the least bit sad or apprehensive about it.

'Have you ever been to France?'

I shook my head.

'Would you like to go there now?'

'Today?'

'Immediately. Are those your bags?'

I nodded and smiled.

He raised a finger to his servant and then pointed them out – two pathetic little cardboard things that made me burn with shame. The man understood his master at once and lifted both easily in one hand.

'Come,' the Comte said and guided me gently toward his coach.

I did not then know he was a French aristocrat; he did not know I was a vicar's daughter with some distant blue blood of my own. Of course, I took the most appalling risk in what I did – but then so did he. It is something one must be prepared to do at certain times – to follow that feeling of absolute certainty that can be as solid

54

within us as any unborn child. The point is that he was wise enough (and I foolish enough) to know it.

That night we stopped at an inn in Dover and I discovered we were to share the same bed and I felt sure I was about to yield him my jewel.

I made what I believed were all the necessary motions. Now that I had seen (or, rather, felt) the size of the Thing that was to break me open (with my curate, I mean – not yet the Comte), I even took a little of the cream that he gave me to rub into my cheeks and smeared it all around my vestibule; it was a strangely pleasing sensation. But he just patted me gently on my hip and said, 'No, no, no, little angel. We have so far to go before we get *there*.'

I thought he meant our journey over the Channel in France. I asked how many days' drive it was on the other side, but he just laughed and hoisted me upon him. It was no easy feat, for I was even then quite tall for my age; but in other ways I was not fully formed at all. My Breasts were just beginning to swell, with the Nipples already large and prominent, quite out of proportion – I was ashamed of them. And my little quim was a pale crescent with a few straggling hairs that I had tried to pluck out, I found them so ugly. I hated what was happening to her, for I thought she had been beautiful in her pearly smoothness. (But you see – I had already started to take an intense interest in those parts; I had stared for hours in fascination at the little folds and rilles of my q., I can assure you.)

My hair was then as lustrous as in my full womanhood but it reached no lower than my shoulderblades. My face was also more babyish – naturally – but when I look back at the portrait the Comte had taken of me at that time, I can see I already had that solemn intensity of mien that Gentlemen have found so beguiling down the years. It was, he said, what attracted him.

55

There are some women, he told me – indeed, he told me as I lay upon him and he caressed me so tenderly at Dover that night – there are some women born to found dynasties between their thighs; others to teach, to partner missionaries in dangerous corners of the globe . . . some to toil in mines or sweat out their miserable lives in laundries and patisseries. 'But there are a few rare creatures, *ma petite chérie*, and I believe you may be one of them, who are born for nothing but Love.'

Now usually when a man says things like that, he means the woman is born to be his plaything. But that was not the Comte's idea at all. Although he knew everything and I nothing, he already believed that I would one day soar far beyond him in my appreciation, and practice, of the Arts of Love – the very Arts he now proposed to teach me, step by careful step. 'How do you feel about this prospect, little gazelle?' he asked me tenderly. 'Do you think me a foolish old man who does nothing but deceive himself – or do you feel ready for that momentous journey?'

I tried to answer him yes but my voice broke on the very first utterance and I could do nothing but weep in silence, and kiss his cheeks, and feel hot with shame, and burn with a strange, unlocatable longing for him, and wish his voice would go on and on in my ear for ever.

And so we fell asleep, my little, naked, young girl's body stretched out and open on his great, muscular frame, which was naked, too. And him so self-controlled and sure of his prowess that not once did his manhood rise to me.

When I awoke next morning we were lying side by side; I had never felt sheets so soft and smooth and warm . . . in short, I had never slept in silk before. But what had awakened me was his hand, which he laid gently in the small of my back and then held still. How did he know that was what I wanted, what I craved above all? Precisely that touch and no other. Precisely that degree of pressure. I felt a languorous warmth radiating outward from it, down over my little *derrière*, down between my thighs and all along their insides until it reached my knees. It caressed the backs of my knees, that unearthly warmth, until I felt that all of me was melting.

My heart beat wildly and there was a disorder in my breathing. I tried to turn to him but at the first tensing of my muscles he increased the pressure of that marvellous hand and I understood I was to keep still. And then he began a gentle massage. He did not rub my skin so much as move it gently over the bone which, in that region – as you know – is so near. And this combination – the firmness of my bones, the softness of my skin, and the almost unbearable energy that seemed to flow out of his hand . . . how can I describe it? Can you imagine vibrations that do not actually move? That is what passed from him to me. As his outspread hand slowly stirred my flesh upon its bone, my innards were suddenly filled with those strange vibrations that threatened to peel me apart.

It was, of course, my first Climax with a man – a trivial, hasty thing compared with the Marathons of Ecstasy he was later to give me, but it had a sweetness and delight altogether different in character from anything I had known before or since. And he wrought it in me, though he did no more than gently move the skin in the small of my back. If ever there was a single moment that bound me to him for life, that was it.

Again I found myself gently weeping, but he chuckled and pushed his fingers down into my cleft, 'Look,' he said, 'here are your real tears. Your sweet little *cutte* is mourning her lost innocence now. You have crossed the Rubicon, little gazelle . . .' And so on. He made me put my fingers down there and feel it for myself.

I must have made a face at what I thought was its

57

unpleasant odour, for he carried my hands at once to his lips and licked them clean. 'There is no perfumier in the world can match the power of that,' he assured me. And thus he began to teach me 'there is nothing in this world, nor good nor bad, but thinking makes it so.'

'Now I feel sure of it,' he said happily. 'You are one of that rare breed of Woman. Your gifts will one day carry you far beyond me. But no matter – I am now a slave of your great talent.'

I thought this the height of foolishness, for if either of us was bound to the other in a slave-master relationship, I felt I was his until the end of time.

Oh, Sweet Fanny, this has disturbed me more than I had bargained for. I thought I had recalled those days so often, down the years, they had lost their power over me. But, as I now discover, it is one thing to recall them in one's fancy – skimping each moment as the mind is so apt to do; it is quite another to set them down like this, syllable by syllable. For I can recall everything, as if it had but happened now, in the next room here – the taste and texture of the apple we shared, bite for bite, at breakfast that day – the tang of the sea water in which I washed my face, for I had never seen or tasted it before and it seemed to me almost erotic in its saltiness. I was suddenly on the hunt for every kind of erotic sensation, though I did not know it until some weeks later, when it all became conscious with me.

However – and as always, I fear – I anticipate what must now be my next letter, for this has wearied me more than I can say. Answer me or not, entirely at your pleasure. This exercise in recall, persuasion, explanation – what you will – has now gained a drive of its own. I find that even *I* wish to learn what I'm going to remember next, and why, and what lesson I draw from it for you. I hang upon my own discoveries.

So many things are becoming clear to me now.

Ever yours, sweet nymph,
Frances
Comtesse de C.

LETTER FIVE

FROM MOUNT VENUS,
Sunday, 24th March, 1850

Sweet Fanny,
 I keep no copies of these letters. Did I say that the motion of our ship made Intercourse of any kind impossible twixt me and the Comte for at least a couple of days after we landed at Calais? Indeed, I believe we arrived here at the Château in T–ne before he and I resumed our cohabitation of the same bed. We did nothing that first night but talk – of the Château and his other lands, of his responsibilities and the havoc left over from the Revolution and the days of the Directoire and Napoleon. He also spoke of his wife, who died almost on the day I had been born, giving birth to their only son; whether the son had

survived he did not say and I was too shy to ask.

Then he began to ask me about myself. Of course, we had already covered the main events of my utterly fascinating life – which had consumed an entire *hour* on the journey down. But now he wanted to know my intimate story – the boys I had known, what I thought of them, and so on. What had I thought when I first saw a penis – any penis . . . horse, dog, bull, or human? What had impelled me to experiment with the curate in that rash way? Had I ever seen my father and my mother *in flagrante*? Or heard them at it when they thought I was asleep? These and many more.

At first, though I answered openly enough, I did not understand his purpose, especially as he did not seem very interested in my replies. But then I saw that he was trying to get me to talk out of myself any guilt or awkwardness I might have felt on these intimate matters. I now realize, too, of course, that he had caught me a year too young to have developed much in the way of shame. (And I hope and pray the same is true of you, dear child. Most of the evils that attend the human condition can be traced back to a quite unnecessary feeling of guilt or shame about something or other – and usually 'other'!)

Anyway, my honest answers seemed to please him and he began to talk of shame as a kind of uninvited guest we might both glimpse from time to time at the outer edges of our developing companionship and whom we should learn at once to shoo away.

'When the weather is warmer,' he told me, 'we all go naked here, in the Château and the private garden.'

'Even the servants?' I blurted out.

'They are humans, too,' he replied coolly, thinking my question snobbish in the extreme.

'It is not that,' I told him. 'But what if they should spill hot soup down their fronts?'

62

He laughed then, and hugged me to him, and told me I had shamed him enough for one day with my innocence. 'The servants do not, in fact, go naked,' he explained. 'I was annoyed at what I thought you were implying.'

'Who then?' I persisted.

'Certain young girls you will see about the place. Pretty little creatures I have brought here from time to time, since my wife died – some of whom have stayed.'

'As you brought me?' I asked, feeling an acute disappointment that I was, as it now seemed, to share him with an entire hareem.

'No,' he assured me. 'There is no one in all the world like you, little gazelle.'

'But you will enjoy them as you no doubt mean to enjoy me,' I grumbled.

'And I promise you, you will not complain.'

I said nothing.

'We are all available to each other,' he added. 'I to them, they to me, us to each other, you to them . . .'

'A girl!' I exclaimed in disgust. 'Available to me?'

He said no more but rolled me on my back and began to caress my nipples. Then, just when I thought I would die of longing for him to do more, he cradled me in his arms and fell at once asleep. I had then the first vague intimation of what he meant when he said I would one day go far beyond him in matters of Love. Despite all his wisdom, all his experience, there was something childlike and immediate in everything he did.

The following day he began my sensual education in earnest. He took me into the library where he pulled out some volumes of erotic prints. I know now that they were not very good, but perhaps that was all to his purpose. He was never of that sybaritic clan which drives itself to distraction in seeking out only the best, the greatest, the biggest, the ultimate. It was always his point that

Life – and the Sensual Life as well as any other – is an entire gamut that we must experience in all its glorious diversity. *L'homme sensuel* is a balanced man who knows the value of the sublime because he has tasted the tawdry, too.

I add all this now to explain why he invited me to sit down and inspect that not-too-inspiriting collection. He said nothing of it at the time, of course. In fact, what he did say was, 'Please unbutton your blouse and expose your beautiful little breasts.'

I, of course, was delighted to comply.

'Now, caress your nipples gently as I did last night.'

'I'd rather it was you,' I replied roguishly.

But he had already vanished beneath the table. A moment later I felt him pushing up my skirts. 'Are you studying the pictures?' came his voice.

'Yes.' I hastily did so.

'And caressing your nipples?'

'Yes.' I began to do that, too.

'Describe to me the sensations you feel.'

'When you touch me, all I feel is you.' He was spreading apart my thighs and pulling off my drawers – even though they were of the open kind, common then, which offered no impediment to sight or touch.

'Talk of that then. And go on caressing yourself, too.'

'I feel a . . . freedom . . . I mean I felt it when you untied my drawstring.'

'What sort of freedom?'

'Delicious,' I said, feeling silly at having to utter the word.

'And now? Don't always wait for me to prompt you. Just talk. Forget it's you that's talking. You're just an observer. Your body is now a battlefield of feelings and thoughts and desires. You're just telling me what's going on.'

And it suddenly occurred to me that if he didn't feel stupid sitting under the table like that, talking to me like a play director, then I certainly ought to feel all right about describing my feelings to him.

He hardly needed to interrupt after that – just to say things like, 'Lean back . . . spread yourself even wider . . . show me all . . .'

No man, of course, had ever kissed those lips down there, nor wrapped his tongue around my bud, yet I knew I found myself longing for him to do both. At first I was ashamed of the thought, despite all he had tried to teach me; but in the end my craving grew so desperate I blurted it out.

Before I had finished, his tongue was there, burrowing away, marvellous in its energy. I gurgled, and lay back in my chair, and began to slide toward him, increasing the pressure, clamping his head between my slim little thighs as I underwent a spasm of delight beyond anything I had thought was possible.

And when it was done, I felt him pull me up. And then I discovered he was now standing behind me, with his hands down over my breasts, showing me what *petits tressaillements* I might discover on my way down. He was no longer the calm teacher, though. His pulse was racing and his speech was far from smooth.

'You go fast and far, little gazelle. I think you will yield up your precious jewel quite soon.'

'Oh please,' I whispered, pulling him down upon me.

I think it was his disorder that made me realize I was a Woman at last. It is a kind of power we cannot help exercising over them. If a Woman walks down the street, they *must* turn and follow her, if only by gaze. We are the flame and they the moth. They die in us and go away to be reborn. But we gather their strength and can give ten for their one.

These are words I put upon it now, of course, half-way through my intended life. At the time I was only aware of an enormous surge of well-being and confidence; I knew I could force him to it that night.

We went to our bed immediately from the table; he had allowed me wine for the first time, in recognition of my gathering status. I didn't like it, but that was beside the point. As with my own intimate aromas, it was an acquired taste. It would come.

We had undressed each other before, but – in that careful schedule of his – in a curiously impersonal way, like turning the pages of one of those books that show a girl undressing bit by bit, as in a zootrope. But now it was hot and urgent – by which I do not mean hasty, for we lingered an age at each garment, pressing a hundred kisses to the flesh its removal had bared, and little love bites, too – and slaps, and giggles, and chases, and catchings.

But at last there we were, down to our drawers and about to face the final revelation, in his case to me. For though I had seen his penis before, I had never seen it so roused and hard as it plainly was beneath those folds of cloth.

He chased me, caught me, plucked at the string of my drawers – and I felt again that freedom I had described to him as delicious. 'My turn now,' I told him. 'You had yours this afternoon.'

He resigned himself to it and stood where he was. I, now nude as a babe, dropped to my knees before him and faced, literally inches away, the cloth whose parting would reveal what I hoped would soon be the bringer of all my joys. He, meanwhile, ran his finger lightly down the parting of my hair. 'You have run so fast, little gazelle,' he murmured sadly, as if he would rather have trotted me on the lunge a further week.

But I was now all afire to have it done. I wanted to

know what that feeling was like. Gingerly, filled with the most awesome premonitions and literally having no idea what I was going to discover, I raised my finger to the slit in his cloth – the one that draws open down the front to let them ease themselves.

His erection moved with it at first – and then it suddenly came bursting out – hot and red and monstrous and gnarled with veins and tight flesh and wrinkled flesh and hair, not just at its base but half-way up it, too. It was . . . bestial . . . vile. Yet I felt a dreadful, contradictory urge to take it in my hands and cover it with kisses. Since then I have often thought that such contradictions are at the heart of all our greatest pleasures. We must first be repelled; but our repulsion must be overcome by some more powerful attractive force. It is the way a cheese with 'noble rottenness' is always more satisfying to the true gourmet than the bland, creamy stuff anyone can make in her own kitchen.

All at once I noticed it was leaping around in the air as if it were alive – I mean, as if it had a life of its own. I did not realize he was doing it deliberately; I did not even know it was possible for a man to do that deliberately. But it was just his way, testing me, putting me to some new limit, just when I had conceived the notion of overcoming my repulsion and putting my lips to its skin.

Absently, almost without knowing it, I tugged at his drawstring, letting his last vestige of clothing fall away. Then I gathered it into my hands and fell upon it with my kisses.

The Comte now led me to our bed where, without a word spoken, he encouraged me to lie between his knees and make all the discoveries I wanted.

And then I laughed, partly at my earlier fears and partly at how strange it felt. There is no other bit of our anatomy, male or female, sweet Fanny, that in any way resembles it in touch and texture, so you must just (I trust) take my word for it. Its skin, believe it or not, for all its gnarled and ill-used appearance, is softer than any part of ours – our dry skin, anyway. When it is flaccid, it is as limp as your tongue, or as your tongue would be if dry. But when it is hard, it is like bone beneath and yet the outer skin remains amazingly supple and elastic.

One of my earliest discoveries that night was that I could grasp the skin at its base, or an inch above, by making a tight ring of my thumb and fingers, and I could pull this up like a shroud until it completely engulfed that great red one-eyed knob at its tip. (The Comte has been circumcized, as you will gather.) And when I let go, out it popped again like a jack in a box! How I laughed!

And then I remembered the pleasure he had given me with his tongue in the library that afternoon, so I thought I would try the same now with him. I hoped he would teach me as he had taught me so many simpler things before; but he implied that the time for words was over. He directed me now as all true Lovers direct each other, by gestures, movements of the hips, sighs, little gasps, and so on. In that way I soon learned that the sensual parts of it are where I told you earlier (didn't I?) – along those parts that always remind me of a fish's gills seen from below. Yes, I recall writing that.

It struck me then that those two downward-sloping swellings of his knob, were amazingly like the two outer lips of my own little q. And I already knew that the rosebud of Pleasure, in my case, was at their very apex – which was how I discovered it in him. When I later told him so, he was amazed. The similarities are no mere accident, he said; the two seats of pleasure are related, in some way he didn't explain (or he probably did but I didn't listen). But he had never known anybody make that discovery in the heat of the moment, as it were.

At the time, all I know is that it near drove him wild as I sucked and licked away. His eyes started in their sockets, his nostrils flared, his breath came in gasps, then all of a sudden the thing was throbbing away like mad and his milt was flying all over everything – the bed, his belly, my face – everywhere, according to the accident of its aim at the time. The most surprising thing was its heat.

I just lay there and watched it in utter fascination. I had read of this event, of course – in most of the books he had shown me over the past few days. I had watched animals in rut in the fields as long as I could remember. And there had been my curate . . . But none of it was any preparation for this manic throbbing and the free-flying milt. Only then did the disappointment hit me – that having spent himself in this futile way (and all my fault!) he would now have nothing left for me inside.

Little did I know my magnificent Comte! He is one of those rare men (I met a few since during my years in the Trade) who can go on and on. It is a kind of voluntary priapism – not that merciless kind which gives a man no ease and puts him in constant pain, but one he can assume at will, in the right spirit and company. I have seen him roger no fewer than . . . but no, I will tell you of that anon.

What he had shot on my face he now massaged in, telling me how good it was for my skin and how it would ward off blemishes. I laughed, thinking it no more than a lover's pleasantry; he did not insist. I never knew him insist on anything – except, perhaps, our absolute right to be ourselves in all things.

Then he patted the sheets beside him, invitingly. And when I lay there, he took up the rest of his milt and gently annointed my hole, which I spread wide in offering to his delicate touch.

'What if it quickens me?' I asked, not wanting to talk about what he was going to do.

'So be it,' he answered simply. 'That is Nature's way. The child will be handsomely provided for.'

'You should not marry me?'

'I shall not marry anybody, ever again.'

His finger found that little button and I began to melt once more. Even then, as that overpowering sense of languor overcame me, I knew what he was doing – trying to make my own juices flow to ease his penetration. So the moment had come at last.

I marvel now at how little I really thought about it all; I just lay there and let myself become one seething mass of pure feelings. Had I given it a moment's contemplation I would have realized at once that my tiny little hole, with her thin veil of hymeneal skin intact, could never in a thousand years accommodate anything as large as that. But the very idea was alien to that mood in me. I just lay there and waited for everything to happen by some miracle. I have read books in which that moment is compared to the way a snake can hypnotize a rabbit – which just sits there, filled with terror yet calmly awaiting its *coup de grâce*. Believe me, sweet Fanny, it was not like that at all. There was not one trace of terror in me; I just knew a miracle was going to happen.

And I did not even know that any other man would have gone limp by now, so *that* miracle had already passed me by.

When I was as wet and gleaming as could possibly be down there, he lifted my *derrière* and pulled a large pillow beneath it. I think the especial delight I always feel when any man handles that part of me with such masterful competence – disposing me just so for his particular Pleasure – can be traced back to that moment with my darling Comte. He spread me wide and held my thighs apart by underpinning them with his own. Then, with the tenderest of motions he bent forward, bringing his knob to rest against my little rosebud of Joy, which he now began to stimulate, with tiny circular movements and brief stabs and thrusts, until I felt so congested I could hardly breathe. It did not help that his fingers now danced with maddening gentleness over my nipples. An almost unbearable thread of pleasure seemed to connect them with something in the pit of my stomach – something that yearned for . . . I knew not what. My whole body turned into one great shout of carnal longing.

And in that sweet delirium I was only vaguely aware when the point of his pressure moved and his knob was pushing, with all the gentleness in the world, at my little veil. Still he kept up that motion, the tiny thrusts, the small gyrations. And so it happened – with none of the drama I had anticipated. My maidenhead yielded, almost at random, to one of those movements of his; I hardly felt it go. Certainly there was not that 'sweet stab of pain' you read about in certain books. One moment it was there; next moment, silently, it had folded up and gone.

It helped that he did not immediately follow up and urge himself indoors. He just went on with the same movements as before, but every now and then – almost as if it were a tiny accident – he would get the very tip of himself inside. Then out again at once.

At last I could bear it no longer. 'Stay in!' I cried when I felt him about to withdraw again.

He stopped moving, with just the tip of him inside. His hands went down to grasp my slim little hips and hold me still for this, the first stretching of love's lane. I gave out one long gasp of delight as he went smoothly in, all the way – not to the hilt of *him* but to the point where he felt I could take no more.

Then he began the slowest poking I ever had, I think; withdrawing himself to the merest tip, letting my flesh relax back in upon itself, and then pressing oh so gently forward again, expanding me, letting me feel what it was like. And then I learned I had other excitable parts – not just that little bud I had discovered some years earlier. And this new excitation was quite different. Where rosebud's thrill was light and serene, this was visceral and profound. When rosebud sang her sweetest I thought I would pass out; when these new, as yet unlocated *tressaillements* seized me, I imagined I might die.

He was still grasping my hips, which I felt was no longer necessary. I wanted the whole weight of him upon me now. I wanted to wriggle beneath him and know I was hopelessly trapped, impaled for ever on that marvellous instrument of my pleasure. I wanted to throw my little legs up around him, to roll over and squirm right into him, to hug every particle of that splendid body inside mine. I only wanted things that were impossible.

I did none of them; I banked them against all our tomorrows in that delicious bed. I just lay there and revelled in the grasp of him and the thrust of him and the miraculous expansions of my mind and body which he had so easily achieved. I did not know I was having climax after climax, for these were so deep inside me I simply thought I had moved on into another country, where sensation was the very air we breathed. Only when he came, and I felt him throbbing like a fury inside me, and gasping for breath, and giving out little whimpers . . . only then did my own pleasure find its focus. And at last I knew what had been going on within me.

From then on that became the Comte's way of teaching me anything new: He let me make my discoveries for myself. He let them happen inside me – now that there was, at last, a true inside where they might lodge. But he always took care to strew my way with clues that I would be sure to pick up as I went.

We slept and loved each other fitfully until dawn,

when we both fell into the profoundest slumber imaginable. My last thought, I remember, was that I must now have tasted everything Cupid and Venus could devise between them for human Pleasure!

Ah me!

Ever yours, sweet nymph,
Frances
Comtesse de C.

LETTER SIX

FROM MOUNT VENUS,
Wednesday, 3rd April, 1850

Sweet Fanny,
 But is it not natural that my memories of my sentimental education, here in our beloved Château, will be different from those of my days as a Lady of Pleasure in London? That time was, after all more than two decades ago, for the most part, between my eighteenth and thirty-second years; and though my tutelage under the Comte was earlier still, between my sixteenth and eighteenth years, it is, in a way, all about me yet. Why, I sit in the very room where the events I am about to relate occurred! If memory grows shy I can glance around and have it refreshed by some small detail – a picture on the wall, a

crack in the ceiling, a knot in the woodwork curiously shaped by Nature in the form of the female q. And so on. I don't think these differences should puzzle you at all. So let me get on with it.

After that night when I at last gave up the burden of my virginity and learned what it was (or so I thought) to be a Woman at last, the Comte deserted me! No – I tease – though that is what it felt like at the time, I assure you. The poor man would rather have continued my sentimental education, day and night, than anything else in the world; but the cares of that world weighed upon him as heavily as my maidenhead had upon me. He had already neglected them too long, so now he was away a century and more. A week, anyway.

I wandered disconsolate about the Château, or the parts of it I could reach. Can you remember it from that brief visit you paid us so many years ago, when your dear mother was so hard up? If so, you will recall how strangely it had been constructed over the years – a number of distinct towers, linked by what, from an external view, seem to be great chambers of state but which, from the inside, are revealed as mere follies, blank walls, architectural stage scenery. The true connections between the towers are all concealed; and when I asked the servants where they were, they replied that the Comte would show me, all in good time. I understood then that I was still a child in their eyes; it was the 'wait and see' answer our old cook used to give me every time I strayed into the vicarage kitchens and asked 'What's for pudding?' Lord, how that infuriated me!

And how it infuriated me now. For, from the upper casements of the only tower I was able to explore I had discovered two others of absorbing interest. One was where he kept that hareem he had mentioned. (I express all these thoughts as they were in my mind at that time.

Of course, when I understood the truth, 'hareem' was the last word I associated with that place. And though, I suppose, the Comte did *keep* us females in the strictly legal sense, the very idea was alien to the freedom that prevailed among us there.) That tower was a little way off but I often saw the girls at their windows, combing out their hair or throwing crusts at the birds – or, sometimes, waving back at me! But I hated them then. I hated the very thought of their existence and the knowledge that they would soon be stealing from the Comte the pleasurable hours that should be mine alone. I always shrank back from my window and slammed it coldly against all their friendly overtures. Oh yes, I was a child.

The other tower was the neighbour of mine – indeed, its twin. And, in a curious way, it seemed to house my twin, as well: a youth of no more than sixteen who lived there with an entirely separate household – and a rather grim one by all appearances. It seemed largely male – tutors and masters of skills as well as the usual footmen etc. The females were all very matronly and severely dressed. I often saw him standing at his window, my little fair-haired twin, gazing intently at that other tower with its much jollier company of girls! But that was before he even knew of my existence.

Don't imagine, however, that I spent long hours at my windows, gazing at that young man and the happy tower of girls! No, my darling Comte had left me plenty to *occupy* myself with! A whole pile of lascivious books, for instance. I found the stories more stimulating than the illustrations. They spanned the entire range of carnal recreation, from the sweetest, tenderest things to acts that even now I do not care to think about. But I read them all, whether they moved me or not, and marvelled at the ingenuity and inventiveness of people when their pleasure is in play.

Certain passages I read and reread. The sort of thing that really 'lit my lamp', as they say, was a good detailed description of a lively couple preparing for their horizontal pleasures. I loved to read of a beautiful young girl being bathed by her handmaidens, then dried, and powdered and perfumed, before being draped in flimsy cottons that were little more than woven air. Or perhaps she would just wear a single gem in a golden setting on a fine gold chain about her waist. Thoughts of gold in proximity to female flesh was always a powerful aphrodisiac to me. My beautiful young maiden being prepared for her night of carnal thrills would be a little apprehensive as to whether her delicate body could withstand the lusty assaults of her vigorous (and, of course, always tireless) young lover; she would doubt that her exquisite and refined nature could tolerate the storms of passion that would begin to surge through her from the moment their eyes met and would then hardly abate before dawn.

Even then I knew (or had the strongest suspicion) that a Woman's body, however delicate, and her emotions, no matter how fine, can tolerate almost anything in the way of voluptuous and sensual pleasure. Much more so than any Man. I felt, as my Comte had said, that I was actually *created* for such Joys, both to give and to receive, but above all to receive them. So why did those descriptions of young maidens experiencing thoughts and feelings quite alien to me nonetheless delight me and fill me with desire? I suppose that, in a perverse but typically feminine way, I was mourning the loss of a kind of innocence I had never in fact possessed.

But, roused I was. And, having no Man about me that week, I had to make do with what the Comte had left me.

The first was a little witticism of his – my Golden Douche. How characteristic of him that it has also been of such practical value, too – my 'spare coach a mile behind'. I have invariably used it at the end of those nights when I have had but one or two lovers, whose milt might form a wily male alliance rather than fight over me. You have never seen it, have you? No, of course not! And I now realize I have never described it, either. Well, it is in the form of a long pego – long compared to its width, that is, about seven inches, but only half an inch in diameter. (A Man would say 'over one and one-half inches round', because that, though the identical measure, makes it sound the larger!) (And, while on the subject of such differences, have you noticed that a Man will talk of a blouse that *opens* down the side while a woman will say that it *buttons up* there?) But back to my Douche. Seven inches? I have just put a tape to it. It is in fact, seven and a half, which, as I was about to say, is just long enough to reach all the way up Love Lane and get his tip in through the mouth of my womb; I have acquired the skill of manipulating it there without discomfort. As an English lady said recently on arriving here in France and seeing her first-ever bidet, 'Oh how sweet! Is it for washing babies in?' And the porter told her, '*Non*, Madame, it is for washing them *out*!' And that is both why and where I use my Golden Douche. The rubber bulb, which I squeeze to expel the wash fluid, is cunningly cast in (you have surely guessed?) the form of a Man's balls – or, rather, the sac or scrotum in which they dangle. Men wince to see me use it in this way, for, indeed, (be warned!) there is no part on *our* bodies so delicate and easy to hurt as that. Naturally, I had little use for it, except to experiment with and laugh at, during that time while the Comte was away.

But I could not say the same of the other engine of amusement he gave me as he left. This, too, was in the shape of a Man's organ but of proper size and girth – six and a half inches long and nearly as many round, if you want it in their terms; a bare two in diameter, if you want it in mine. I believe it was Oriental, carved in ivory and realistic in every detail – but with the addition of a series of fine rings all down its length. These were part of the carving, not added after, and they ran up and down all the natural contours of the thing – the puckered remnants of the foreskin, the veins, and so on – most ingenious. But its miraculous outer detail was the least of its wonders. The scrotum, which also provided its handle, housed a clockwork motor that drove a tiny hammer – or piston, or something. Anyway the effect was to make it vibrate ten times as fast as your most skilful finger. I'm sure you understand me?

This superb toy, when brought to blood heat and a little more by standing carefully in hot water, gave me hours of delight that long, lonely week – and occasionally over the years that followed, too. Looking back now, I can see that its great value was that it allowed me to discover so much about my erotic parts – where the finest thrills were hidden, and all their different kinds. I must have explored a hundred times the difference between the joys that flowed from my Rosebud and those that lay deeper inside Love Lane. At the time, of course, it did not seem like learning at all, I just lay in bed or sat on my sofa or chair or stood and leaned dreamily against a wall, and drowned myself in these amazing new sensations. I learned how I could prolong the ecstasy by letting it decline and then, as it were, *rushing* it up again with a deep insertion of that marvellously living tool. Or I could keep myself, almost forever it seemed, on a lower plateau of delight by rubbing it over my bud every once in a while.

I would awaken in the mornings already reaching for it and would have to seek ways of prolonging my arousal. First I would think about it, and the different ways I had learned in its use. Had I discovered them all? Were there parts of my body I had neglected, where new sensations might be lurking in wait for that magical release? My nipples? My mouth? In the pits of my arms? Behind my knees, where I so often felt a special kind of melting weakness when the Comte but touched me? Little Miss Brown, even? I tried them all and discovered there were, indeed, such places. In fact, after some days my lusts were aroused to such a fever that I could stroke almost any part of my skin and it would evoke some sort of thrill.

That, then, was my condition when the Comte returned. Oh, I think my heart shivered into a dozen pieces and leaped into every part of my body when I heard his carriage thunder over the drawbridge. I thought he would come rushing upstairs, tear every stitch from my back, and ravish me where I stood. But it was an hour before I saw him. How I raced into his arms and clung to him! But, after embracing me warmly enough and covering my neck and lips with kisses, each one of which left me more molten than ever, he pushed me gently away and said, 'Let us eat.'

I almost cried out my disappointment, but I saw that gleam in his eye which promised it would be so much better for waiting a little longer, and thus I contained myself, if only just.

I remember nothing of that meal. I cannot believe I managed to eat much, and he, for once, did not insist. He always held that fine food was essential to the enjoyment of our carnal appetites; people who lived on lard and meal could know nothing of Love – all they did was . . . well, I cannot say it without using the crudities of whores, which I never shall do. (But the equivalent word in English describes something like a *nail* and it rhymes with *stews*, which is where it belongs.)

He, to be sure, dined well, occupying me by asking

how I had passed the time. I told him – everything – almost as I have related it above, except that I was still intoxicated by my discoveries and brimming over with my craving for him. At first he was merely amused at my enthusiasm, then pleased; but when he saw how intense a passion it had awakened in me he became troubled, and I felt again that power we Women have over even the most suave and self-controlled of men. My yearning was like a furnace that shrivelled up his urbanity and brought him to face that carnal beast beneath his own skin – the creature he liked to keep on leash until we were well settled to our loving, naked and with the perspiration already flowing. It could not live among gold plate and *crème brulée*; his finely embroidered damascene waistcoat could not contain it. I saw that my overpowering femininity was upsetting some carefully laid plan for tonight's revels.

'Come!' He rose hastily and wiped his lips, throwing the napkin to the floor in his haste.

I thought he would take me to our bed, but his way led down. Even when we reached the ground floor, still it went down – and then I realized I had now passed beyond the first *niveau* of my sentimental education – what one might call its solo phase, which every young girl must undergo, though few so thoroughly as I! – and was now, both literally and figuratively entering the second.

What was it to be? I felt sure he was taking me to the tower where the young man (as I liked to think of him, though he was, in fact, barely a youth) lived. For what purpose? Had he fattened my desires as a housewife fattens her geese – to feed to others? Was I now to pass on my small learning to that young fellow? I was amazed to find that the idea only added to my excitement. If the suggestion had been put before me earlier, in a cooler mood, as it were, I would have said a thousand times no! For then I was sure I burned with my craving for one man alone – my dear, darling Comte. But now, as long as he was at my side, I found the idea of experiencing another man's (or male's) embraces was, if anything, more exciting still. If he had inherited his father's nature (I was as certain as could be that this was the only son, whose mother had died in childbed), I could pass from one to the other all night long; and I was sure, from my experiments with that ivory engine, that I at least would not flag now.

But it was to *that* tower he took me. Could he read my mind? I think not, though there was always some powerful sympathy between us that could move us to do almost identical things at the identical moment. He never had a climax within me, for instance, without my matching him, spasm for spasm; but then I would have had a dozen on the way there, so that signifies less than it might. And half a dozen afterwards, too.

No, I believe he had asked the servants to note what books I read while he was away and to mark particularly those passages to which I returned. I say this because the moment we emerged into that other tower, the tower of the happy young girls, I found two of them waiting to conduct me to my toilette! They were clad in the flimsiest of gowns, so opened at the front that their breasts were naked. One, who was introduced to me as Elaine, had a tiny gold locket hanging between hers; Garence, the other, had a fine chain of gold – no setting, no gem – around her waist, gathering in the delicate material of her gown and showing how slender she was.

And oh, what beautiful breasts they had, Sweet Fanny! I thought of my own pathetic little swellings and felt sick with shame. And though both were slim and graceful, all their curves were fully formed, compared with my still-girlish angularities. And their *emboscage*, too, which the delicate weave of their gowns did little to hide, were luxuriant . . . and, I suddenly noticed, carefully plucked into the form of little hearts! Again, I thought of my own straggly moss . . . and if I had had a dagger about me, I think I would have plunged it into the Comte's back for doing this to me.

They must have known how I felt, petite Elaine and svelte Garence; had they not once dwelled there, too – in that dreadful country where the mind and desires of a woman are forced to live in the bodies of children? But they knew what the Comte wanted – that hateful, odious ogre, as I now thought of him. (Well, perhaps my memory exaggerates as little. It was an evening of wild, disordered feelings that surged and stormed within me; so whatever I say is bound to fix it too firmly in one direction or another. Just remember that if I seem to contradict myself in what follows.)

What followed, in fact, was that the Comte vanished while I was falling from sublime joy to abject dismay. Elaine and Garence took me gently by my arms, one each, like the gaolers they were, despite their gossamer touch, and led me up the staircase, I knew not where. Elaine, too, was English but we all spoke French – as I always did with the Comte. Perhaps I should have explained that earlier; I too readily assume you know all about us, when, of course, you know so little.

'You must be feeling a little nervous?' Elaine asked me.

I stared at her, so pretty with those stupendous auburn tresses tumbling freely down to her waist. She must have seen that 'nervous' was not the most apt word to describe my emotions; I promise you – by now the last shreds of carnal craving had subsided within me. I just wanted to get away from that place and run and run and never stop or see any of them again. But all she did was smile sweetly and say, 'I envy you'.

I knew at once that she was trying to provoke me into asking why, so I turned to Garence, who was the palest blonde I had ever seen – short of an actual albino. Her hair was the colour of the finest silver-gilt. 'Me, too,' she said with that same encouraging smile.

I snorted and looked straight ahead.

Elaine went on speaking, anyway. 'The first time a girl enjoys love with M. le Comte in the Main Guard is heavenly enough – though you know that already, don't you. But her first time in *this* place is altogether out of this world.'

When she has breasts like pigeon's eggs? I thought angrily. *And bones all over the place? And a bush that wouldn't hide an ant?*

You may imagine how I resisted their attempts to disrobe me! But it was no good. The room to which they had conducted me was almost entirely taken up by a large sunken bath, all in marble, and filled with steaming-hot water that gave off the most powerful aroma of cedar. They quickly abandoned their attempts, not wishing to start on a fight, and seeing how determined I could be when I wanted, and instead slipped off their gowns and, with their arms around each other's waists, descended step by step into that inviting water. Their intimacy contrasted so powerfully with my sense of isolation – of being outside some delightful sisterhood – that I almost broke down and wept. Well, at least it was a softening of my rage, though it did nothing to restore my happiness.

Once in the water they swam about and splashed each other and laughed – and paid me no heed at all. That made it easier for me to take that essential first step, which I realized I had no means of avoiding – to shed my clothes and join them. They laid off their games and welcomed me with hugs and kisses. And I must confess – whether it was the heat, or the delicious feeling of hot water against my skin, or the fragrance of cedar, or our bodies wriggling so casually in and out of contact – my anger suddenly vanished in all that steam. Then I swam and splashed and laughed with them both, and they had the good sense not to treat it as a petty victory nor to show any surprise at all.

It seemed odd to me that we did nothing to protect our hair from the water; but then I did not realize how long our preparations were going to take. From the bath they led me to a much smaller room, where there was a second pool, of cold water this time. They plunged in at once, amid squeals of shock that did nothing to encourage me to join them. But join them I did, and added squeals of my own, for now that I had my foot in the door of their sisterhood I was determined not to retreat. 'Why?' I asked when we were out again, and shivering all over.

Garence stretched out an arm and ran her fingers down her fine skin. 'It takes away the strawberries,' she said simply.

'Besides,' Elaine added, 'we'll soon be in the warm again and it'll feel so good.'

They were right, of course. The next room, although it was summertime, had the additional heat of a small porcelain stove whose top was warm to the touch but not hot; it was used for heating the various oils and lotions that were all part of tonight's preparations. It was all exactly as I had read! And I tell you this, Sweet Fanny, it was the strangest thing. But I, who never before or since entertained such misgivings in her life, I began to wonder, as I faced this night of carnal thrills, whether my delicate young body could withstand the lusty assaults of my vigorous (and, as I knew, tireless) lover . . . and whether my exquisite and refined nature could tolerate the storms of passion that would begin to surge through me from the moment we were together again, and which would then hardly abate before dawn!

86

Ah, that is enough for one tired old lady for *this* night. I will write to you very soon, telling more – telling all! – I promise.

Ever yours, sweet nymph,
Frances
Comtesse de C.

LETTER SEVEN

FROM MOUNT VENUS,
Sunday, 7th April, 1850

Sweet Fanny,
We had just emerged from our cold plunge, hadn't we, and into that room where it was warm and filled with the most fragrant aromas. Garence and Elaine took me straight to a pile of hot towels with any one of which you could have dried off a carthorse. I was absolutely *lost* inside mine. But they would not let me dry myself – indeed, from now on, I understood, I was to be the queen and they the handmaidens. I must not lift a finger to do anything for myself. They made it seem like a game, but we all knew that this ritual, which is so well known down the ages, and which must go back to the very beginnings

of erotic civilization, was an important step in my arousal before tonight's revels were joined.

It started the moment they put their hands to my towel and began to rub me dry. There was no laughter now, nor any more girlish chatter; we lived and moved in a voluptuous silence, concentrating on my body . . . on their bodies (for they anointed each other, too, after they had seen to me) . . . and on that congregation of intricate and fleeting sensations that seemed to flash among us like electricity.

When I was dry they sat me on a *fauteuil* of red velvet, and combed out my long, dark hair, following up with a smaller towel; it remained damp, of course, but at least it would dry straight. As they worked they dipped their combs in some lotion that left a delicious musky odour behind. Elaine, being auburn, had that same muskiness as her gift from Mother Nature. (Did you know that? All redheads have it, and it can drive men to distraction – those who can smell it, that is. The rest of us must bless the *parfumier*.)

Our next port of call was something of a shock to me – a marble-lined room to one side of the main chamber with two footstands and a dark hole in its centre – a daily sight to anyone who has lived in France. There they made me bend over and present Miss Brown for their inspection – indeed, more; for Elaine at once inserted an ebony douche and irrigated her out.

'This is God's little joke against Eros,' she told me as I squatted over the hole and let it run out.

'In what way?' I asked in my innocence.

'Putting the two doors so close . . . making them part of the same delicious offering . . .'

Even then I did not twig.

Then they took me back to the main chamber, to a corner, where they stood me over a warm marble slab and began to powder me delicately from head to foot, one working behind, the other in front. (Each of these services, as I said, they also performed for one another; I just stood and watched – and yet again envied their full-grown charms.) The feather-light touch of their powder puffs gave me the most gorgeous feelings, which they knew very well. I remembered my exclamation of disgust to the Comte that I might share erotic feelings with another *girl*. No wonder he had smiled, for how could he have told me it would be as amiable and sensual as this?

Part of that corner was a raised dais, also of warmed marble, about eighteen inches off the ground, with soft pads for kneeling on either side. They caused me to lie down on this, face down at first, while they began to apply little dabs of perfume here and there – to the nape of my neck, the tips of my shoulder-blades, my spine, the small of my back, the tucks of skin at the base of my *derrière*, the backs of my knees, and even my ankles! Each one was given a different aroma, fruity here, rosy there, spicy, savoury, balmy . . . they wrote on my skin a whole landscape of fragrance. And then they turned me over and did the same with my front and up the insides of my thighs – but not, I was surprised to discover, in that most important place of all. Then I recalled the Comte's remark that no *parfumier* in the world could match its natural odour.

Having dealt with their own bodies in a similar way they next took up a pale unguent with no scent at all and with it began to massage my nipples – which, as always, became engorged and firm at once. This proof of my arousal delighted them, and I heard the first laughter since we had begun.

Then I was obliged – or, rather, enchanted – to do the same for them. And in that way I understood that our preparations were already drawing to an end and that our revels, by overlapping them, had actually already begun. Then they laid me back upon the dais and, parting my thighs and spreading them wide, annointed my delicate little *cutte* with the same odourless cream. I closed my eyes and yielded to the pleasure of those slithering fingers, which seemed to know my every cranny better than my own. But I opened them wide again when the fingers went on down that division and lubricated the skin around Miss Brown – and inside her, too, where the irrigation had left her clean and sweet.

'You never know,' Elaine said with the sort of grin that promised *she* did.

And then I twigged.

'Don't pretend to be so shocked,' Garence chided. 'D'you think we can't tell that a certain very interesting engine of ivory has been in here before us – and recently, too!' And she stuck in the tip of her thumb and gave me the most delicious little wriggle.

They laughed to see me blush.

I was not obliged, though again I would have been enchanted, to do the same for them. As I rose from the slab, feeling all warm and melted where they had worked, they took my place and, lying facing inwards, head to foot, with the upper thigh held as vertical as possible, began to work away at each other while I watched in fascination.

The stimulation was too much for them. Almost in unison they each gave a little moan and moved their heads nearer, nearer . . . now resting, cushioned on the lower thigh . . . until, finally, they lay clamped in a feast that, while it undid all their artificial lubrication, swiftly replaced it with something more copious and natural.

This was not part of the due order for the evening, for when I, eager to take part in some way, put my hands between them to caress their breasts, they remembered themselves and sprang apart. Panting heavily with a passion that could not be so quickly stilled, they laughed and stared gratefully at me for my rescue. A few last touches made good the ravages of our excitement, and then we put on our robes. That is to say, we each put on a single garment, and one we could not possibly have worn for any other purpose. I shall describe mine to you, for, colour apart, it was identical to theirs. Elaine's was a sort of pinky fawn – the colour of young mushroom gills; Garence's was dark gray, which showed the rose pallor of her skin to perfection. Mine was a mysterious sort of blue that veered toward purple here and green there – a shot effect, though the weave was far too transparent for that to be its cause.

My shoulders were bare except for the two frilly straps from which the whole garment hung. The frills grew larger and more numerous as they fell down my chest so that, although the hem was cut to bare my breasts, the delicate frills, swinging back and forth, hid and revealed them by turns. The cloth – really it was more like a fine, silken gauze that completely revealed everything it might have been supposed to cover – was gathered into the rather high waist that was still fashionable at that time in France, just three inches or so below the bosom. But the reason for it had nothing to do with fashion. At the back, the hem of the skirt reached to just below my knees, but as it came round to the front it rose in a dramatically curved, upside-down vee whose apex was a tantalizing inch or two below my Venus mound. And there was the only concealment the entire garment had to offer, for, scattered around and above that apex, were little embroidered roses and daisies, clumped tighter together the nearer they reached that focus.

Our very last touch – and a delicate and thrilling one, too – was to lightly rouge each other's nipples, working the blood-red powder gently into the lotion already there. Oh, I think we were ready for a regiment by then! With me in the middle, my arms tight about their waists as theirs were about mine, we slipped into our sandals, took four brief steps across the corridor, and entered a room that had come straight out of the Arabian Nights.

The Comte, arrayed in the gorgeous brocades and embroideries his grandfathers had worn (but not powdered and peruked like them, I'm glad to say), sat cross-legged in the pose of a pasha, in the middle of a vast sea of silken cushions. They spilled upward over an enormous divan behind him, against which he partly lay.

Only then did I notice that his *arbor vitae* was already out and free, and winking at us with its one beady eye. (The pantaloons of that former age had a gusset in the front, you may remember, which made this very easy.) Garence, as if it were a kind of courtly greeting, went down on her knees in front of him and kissed it before snuggling herself against his side. Elaine did the same, snuggling herself against his other side. I bent and kissed it, too, and then, having no side left to snuggle, lingered there, running the tip of my tongue all over it. My two sisters laughed at this, and it struck me that there was something of relief in the tone of it. Perhaps they had feared I would be gauche and awkward, having to be coaxed into things that were second nature to them by now. Its effect on me was to double my resolve to show them I was no longer a child, despite my lack of physical development.

Together they reached down and, taking me by the shoulders, pulled me up until I lay full length upon him. Thinking back on it now, I feel sure that that is where I acquired my passion for lying naked on a man (for I was as good as naked there) in a gorgeous uniform of some kind. Did I tell you about that with dear Commander . . .

what did I call him? André? No – Felix. If not, I should have done.

The two girls left the Comte's embrace and set about assisting the pair of us; so the question that had hovered at the back of my mind ever since we had entered – which of us first, and how do three manage it? – was answered, in part at least. They gently eased me upward to the point where my breasts just hung over the Comte's lips. He did not move at all, except to suckle and kiss and lick them, sending great waves of electricity through me. One of them then closed my knees around his tool and I felt her hand linger there, caressing the hot red knob of it and tickling my thighs in passing.

Soon – everything happened too soon for me, but that was part of the game – they eased me down again, parting and closing my thighs, letting me feel the heat and pressure of his tool as it worked it way up toward my centre of joy. I supposed they would help it in, too, but no, they simply (I say 'they' because if I put a name to it I would just be guessing; I was already half into a delirium where even my own name meant nothing) . . . they simply pressed it against that vertical smile . . . pressed and relented, pressed and relented. The thumb of the hand that was doing all this was curled into a second knob that thrust gently in and out of Miss Brown, too – a fraction of an inch, no more.

I think they were surprised that even these simple pre-liminaries produced in me a climax of earthshaking dimensions – at least, it seemed to shake the earth beneath *me*. They had no idea then what a gargantuan carnal appetite was mine – nor could they have guessed at my capacity to satisfy it. Even I was only beginning to realize it, and also to understand it was something quite rare.

They let me subside before they lifted me off. Then they guided me up onto the divan, where they turned me on my back and bent my knees, so that the delicate embroideries parted and showed my all. Garence immediately buried her head there, her silver-gold hair flowing out over my tiny hips and spilling down onto the dark red silk of the divan. Immediately the most wonderful commotions invaded me. There was no sensation that she was *doing* anything, but little whirlpools of delight spun round and round, deep inside me and all down the backs of my thighs.

A moment later Elaine's slim knees were eased beneath my shoulders and her pale slightly freckled thighs lay each side of my head. I caught that musky tang no *parfumier* could match – and this was the special, heady musk of the redhead, which now drove me wild. Her hands went down and pushed aside the frills that covered my breasts, which she began to rake inward, inward, from their fringes to their tips, oh so delicately that I thrust my chest upward to increase her touch. And then I saw her purpose, for that tilted my head until my eyes were almost buried in her *cutte*. I opened my mouth and half put out my tongue, which was all the invitation she needed to ease herself forward and let me try on her what Garence was doing so successfully with me.

In that heady, musky dark, my body – my person – seemed to float off in all directions. Below my navel revolved one great whirlpool of delight. Above my neck I was in a strange new pasture where nothing I had ever experienced before could guide me on. And in between, the now disembodied caressing of my breasts was a sharp, sweet pleasure all its own – one that held the other two apart, only adding to my utter disorientation. I think I was three separate climaxes now, not one.

But all this was a mere show, to stimulate the Comte while he completed his *déshabille*. In any other circumstances, it would have made me cry out in dismay that I was not allowed to discover him, inch by inch, savouring the texture and flavour of him until it craved for me; but that night the thought did not even cross my mind – indeed, by then, I hardly had mind enough left to cross. I only became aware that he was naked when I felt him at my side, turning me on mine – away from him so that my little *derrière* was spooned in his groin. Garence must have folded up the long back of my gown, for I was naked against him there. She and Elaine had melted away at his touch.

I no longer opened my eyes to see what was happening around me; I was already awash with too much sensation. I just lay there, drowning in their skill, letting them do whatever they wished with me. The Comte hugged me tightly from behind, but only to turn on his back, so that I now lay on top of him, my legs slightly apart and his tool back between them, renewing the only contact it had so far enjoyed of me. Now I discovered where Garence was, for her hot, busy little mouth was working on him, wetting his knob and thrusting it against me with powerful surges of her tongue. At first I thought that was her purpose, but then I realized where she was trying to make it go. Then I shifted the cage of my hips, and wriggled this way and that . . . and then, for the second time in my young life (or the second night, anyway) I had a Man swelling Love's Lane with that most marvellous expansion of all.

But Garence did not stop. As the Comte thrust slowly in and out of me, she moved up and plastered that lovely soft warmth of hers around my bud.

I wondered where his hands had gone; I wanted to feel them around my breasts. But I had forgotten Elaine. She now bent over our two heads, side by side, hanging those gorgeous soft breasts of hers like ripe fruit upon our lips. The Comte gave out a great sigh of satisfaction and began to suckle her nipple and tease it with little bites and licks – as, indeed, did I with the one she had offered me. At the same moment her lips closed around my right nipple and one of her beautiful, tormenting hands started playing with my left. The other hand roamed freely over my stomach and hips, trying to provoke me into dying of pleasure.

Even then I learned we were not done with the Joys we could induce in one another's flesh. The Comte took my hands and raised them above me – beneath Elaine's crouching body. She had been kneeling up until now, more or less in the position in which I had grazed in her *cutte*; but the moment she felt him put me there she rose and knelt over us, doggy-fashion, as they say. I needed no further instruction now. My right hand, with its skilled fingers, went straight where my tongue and lips had been. My other snaked up and around her, to rake the skin of her back with my nails, making her squirm in an agony of pleasure.

And finally the Comte's hands went down to my hips, which he seized in his manly grip and began to caress as only he knew how. I believe I have told you enough, Sweet Fanny, about what sensations that sort of handling always induces in me, so you will believe me now when I tell you that if ever I enjoyed (and I almost wrote 'endured' there, it was so close to pain) . . . if ever I enjoyed a series of climaxes that brought me close to death from their surfeit, that was it. I have felt close to it many times since – more times than I could possibly count – for that is the most agreeable feature of the life of a Lady of Pleasure, the endless supply of lusting men who are willing to pay us for the privilege of trying to procure so marvellous an exit from Life's scene. Had I not come so *truly* close to it that night, those later brushes might, by their fright alone, have finished me off. But that night I truly thought I would never survive it.

I know the Comte spent within me – I mean, I had the copious proof of it long after he withdrew – but at the time I felt nothing, was aware of nothing, except that I had quit my body entirely and was floating in electricity.

I'm sure Elaine and Garence expected me to take no further part that night; indeed, I suspect they had done so much to intensify my ecstasy, partly in hope of getting me out of the way so that they, more experienced in voluptuousness than I, could have our lover to themselves. I saw more than one wide-eyed look at the speed with which I recovered and sought to do for them what they had done for me – and the relish with which I did it (for my suspicions about them had planted within me the germ of a devilish idea of retaliation).

He enjoyed Elaine next, almost immediately after withdrawing from me, as if they were afraid he might go off the boil. Their idea was for Elaine and me simply to change places, leaving Garence where she was. But I pretended to misunderstand and, since it wasn't worth explaining or pushing me off, I managed to take Garence's place instead. There I used my tongue and lips to such good effect that I had Elaine crying out, 'Oh! Oh! . . .' and 'Stop!' in a sort of surprised rapture, long before the Comte was ready. Of course I did no such thing; I merely added the raking of my nails up and down the backs of her thighs – which was something that Garence, thank God, had not thought of doing to me.

But what a fright I got! She went into the most terrible convulsions just as the Comte began spending into her, and I truly suspected I had killed her, or turned her into one of those pathetic creatures who linger on in asylums for years, their brains exploded and vacant. But when the Comte realized what was happening, he pulled away from her and asked in the tenderest tones if she had been taken ill; and his gentleness had the effect of soothing her and aiding her revival. She murmured faintly that she'd soon be all right, and then she just lay there, a little apart from us, panting and shivering.

We all paused then and drank a little sherbet and looked into each other's eyes and smiled at the wonder of life and Love. At least, that was the wonder in my mind. I fancy there was something more complicated going on in theirs. It was the first outside confirmation I'd had of my growing suspicion that my capacity for carnal delight was truly something beyond the ordinary. You'll laugh at the comparison, but the last time I'd seen that look in people's eyes was when little Jimmy Renton joined my father's choir. Through nervousness he had sung badly at his first practice, but – as I'm sure even you'll know, although it is many years since he sang in public – he went on to grace St Paul's and gave concerts that delighted thousands before his voice broke. The power and purity of that astonishing treble was apparent even at his second or third service with our little choir at home. And I remember how people, learned people who knew everything there was to know about music, stared at each other in wonder when they realized what had suddenly come amidst them. Well that was how those three (Elaine, when she recovered), who knew all there was to know about the Arts of Love, looked at each other when they realized what a prodigy of carnal force had now come (and come and come and come!) amidst *them*.

So we returned to our cavorting. It seemed that whatever the Comte did with one he must do with all; it was a sort of sexual democracy among us. Garence therefore took up the position that first I and then Elaine had enjoyed with him. I thought, having seen what I had done to Elaine, she would refuse to let me take the lower office, but I think her curiosity piqued her – or perhaps she thought she was made of stronger sinew . . . anyway, she smiled at me warmly and begged me to stay there.

I did for her exactly what I had done for Elaine, except that her bud was larger, softer, more diffuse, so my movements were more languid as I sought out her especial pleasures. Of course, I hadn't enough experience then to know that was exactly what she wanted anyway, but her shrill of *Oh*! and her deep-throated *Ah*! and her entreaties to me to stop soon told me I was right. Then the Comte tapped my forehead, twice, and unnecessarily hard, I considered; I was going to relent anyway. Even then, Garence's climax was, I gathered, more convulsive than usual for her. There was a sort of wondering, melting look in her eye as she and the Comte separated. He had not spent in her, I was sure; but, after two climaxes in such short order, it would be a heartless girl indeed who would demand more of him than her own release. Certainly G. did not complain.

After another little rest we went at it again, all four. Now there were no what you might call 'set-piece' couplings. I was so excited by what I had done to my two sisters (and, to be sure, by the exercises I had enjoyed all that week) I could by now provoke my climax at will, just as the Comte could maintain his erection – or regain it after our rests – for as long as we had need of it. And so he would pass from one to the other of us, sometimes taking all three of us in turn, giving us ten seconds each, sometimes lingering in one of us as he felt us coming nearer a crisis . . . taking us from behind . . . kneeling . . . lying . . . standing – there was no variation we did not try between us.

And I think my own unbridled excitement was something of a contagion to the other two, for I often caught them looking at each other in a kind of disbelief, with eyes that asked, 'Is this really us? When have we ever enjoyed such lust as this before?' Like me – perhaps through me – they had learned to live on that plateau of rapture where just two or three strokes of a man's tool, or a few brief wriggles from a skilled tongue on their buds, would spill them over into that chaos of indescribable sensations.

The Comte ought to have found his work easier than usual, for he hardly needed to enter any of us before we were gasping and crying stop. At one stage, I remember, we were all three doggo before him, bent almost double with our heads on the cushions and our gorgeous *derrières* waving invitingly at just the right height for him, kneeling behind us. And all he needed to do was give me one poke – that first thrust whose stretching of my little hole is always so thrilling – and I'd melt with a *petit tressaillement* – and so he'd pass on to Elaine, and with just one or two pokes it would be the same for her – and so on to Garence, where, once again, the little miracle would happen – and so back to me to begin once more. That, helped by countless little variations of what he did with his hands, whether he reached in under us and cupped our breasts, or ran his fingernails down our spines, or wriggled the tip of his thumb in Miss Brown (and one or twice it wasn't his thumb, I'm sure!) – whatever it might be – with such little variations he kept us there, up on that sunny upland, for almost twenty minutes.

I say it ought to have been easy work for him since our pleasure would surge through us girls for so much less effort on his part. But alas that sort of rapture cannot be confined, and he, too, was caught up in its infection, so that he spent more copiously than ever. And when he had nothing left to put in us, the pain of it – for him – became too much to bear. And finally, in self defence, that amazing tool, which none of the girls had ever known to flag, fell limp between his thighs. Then there was nothing left to do but curl up together in a delicious entanglement of exhausted limbs, pull a great sheet of embroidered silk over us, and fall into the sleep of the dead.

I was awake an hour later and slipped down underneath the sheet to take the Comte's little acorn of a tool between my lips and try to revive its powers. But all he did was groan and tuck it away between his tight-clamped thighs (making himself look like a woman if there had still been light to see by) and push me away like an annoying little puppy. I moved over to Elaine, but she turned her back and wriggled away from me whatever I tried to do. And Garence was the same. So I just lay there among them, aroused by my efforts and unable to sleep, biding my time.

I did not mind. There was so much to think about and remember, so much to work out, so many new sensations to relate to the old. Even then I think I began to worry about how I would ever be satisfied with just one man. The Comte was quite exceptional in his ability to go on gratifying us girls, but . . . as I had just proved . . .

Elaine got up to relieve herself toward dawn and I asked if I could go too, pretending not to know the way. When we had finished and were just starting on our way back I collided with her and put my arms about her to steady myself. We were still wearing our gowns, by the way; not once in all our exertions had we needed to take them off. I shivered with longing for her – though it would have been the same with Garence or the Comte just then. I was just a living, breathing appetite that even those hours had not managed to quench. 'Oh, Elaine,' I murmured. 'I want you so desperately. Can't you feel it?'

'You are amazing,' she said, but I could feel her starting to tremble, too.

'I've never done any of these things before. I did not

think such pleasure was possible. What can I do? What can I do?'

She hugged me tighter still. 'Come,' she whispered. 'We'll go to my room.'

'The other two won't mind?'

She chuckled. 'I'm sure they'd pay you to go!'

Her room was one floor up. As we mounted the stairs I slipped behind her and began running my hands all over her back and *derrière* and down in between her thighs. 'You are so beautiful and voluptuous,' I told her. 'I hope I grow up to be like you.'

'Oh little one, little one,' she sighed. 'Don't you know the boot is on the other foot? I'm the one who will hope to grow up like you! What on earth will you be in the flower of your womanhood?'

'I want us to be naked together,' I said. 'Just like I saw you and Garence.'

She pressed herself to me, face to face, and for a moment we just swayed softly together, our bodies moving slightly under the gauze of our gowns. I would never have believed that another woman's flesh could be so sensual to me – more so, in some ways, than a man's. I tugged the fronts of our gowns up an inch or two, so that the little bits of embroidery took their *congé* of our mounds and left them in naked congress – her luxuriant bush, my fuzzy little cleft. Again we swayed a little, rubbing ourselves gently together. She gasped. I felt myself melting away. My knees trembled. 'I cannot stand up much longer,' I told her.

She took hold of our gowns, both at the straps, and pulled them up and over our heads and away. That, I realized, was the liberation my body had craved all this while. My next climax – or series of climaxes, if that was to be the way of it – would release me at last. We fell upon the bed and then upon each other, exactly as she

104

and Garence had done during our preparations. Her glorious, rich muskiness had revived in the last few hours and now I gorged upon it to bursting. We began to moan and gasp almost the moment our tongues found each other's buds.

I was well up toward my plateau when I felt a new sensation. At first I could not think what it was; then I realized – she was working her thumb and one of her fingers into my two holes down there. It was one of the most thrilling things I had ever experienced, exquisite rather than profound. I felt it might help to hold me back from one of those deep, earth-trembling climaxes that would end this beautiful feast at once. With a bliss like that, which kept me in a perpetual state of tingling, fluttering liquefaction, it could go on as long as we chose.

Perhaps, I thought, it would do the same for her. I brought my hand round and did as she was doing. Dawn was breaking, so I was just able to see my work. I could dimly make out her two holes, so alike and yet so different, and I found myself picturing the Comte's tool, slowly entering the one, then equally slowly withdrawing, then the other . . . then back to the first . . . and so on. I thought of all the times he must have flown in and out of there, and how the pleasure of it had never palled for her. How long had she been here? Ten years, perhaps? Ten years, richly packed with such nights as this – and still the desire for it beckoned her with an imperative she could not ignore. What unimaginable raptures, then, must still lie ahead of me!

My thumb was doing what I had imagined for the Comte's tool – with the bonus of a little wriggle when it was in full depth, something not even his magnificent engine could achieve. A thousand miles away I heard Elaine gasp and then her ecstasy hit her like a wave. Mine came over me almost at once, too. But that gasp had been almost a giggle, and thus I knew our mutual bliss was of that shallow, honeyed kind we could prolong at our will.

As, indeed, we did, resting and starting again until the sun crept up, sometimes *soixante-neuf*, as that head-to-foot position is called, and sometimes face to face, kissing and wriggling as man and wife would do – and, being so firmly on our two plateaux, we were able, by the slightest pressure, the gentlest little squirm, to climax yet again.

At last she gave up, exhausted. 'Oh – I have never come so many times . . .' (I translate her usage in French, which, of course, I had not heard until that night: '*Je ne suis jamais arrivée . . .*') 'I did not know it was even possible.'

'Just one more,' I pleaded.

We lay together, spoon fashion, on our sides and she put her arms around me from behind and caressed my nipples and breasts and fingered my little button down there and at last brought me that grand release I had craved for . . . how long?

For all my life, it seemed.

Ever yours, sweet nymph,
Frances
Comtesse de C.

LETTER EIGHT

FROM MOUNT VENUS,
Sunday, 21st April, 1850

Sweet Fanny,

This is the letter I have been dreading to write ever since I took up my pen. I knew it would have to come and I knew I should not baulk at it . . . yet even now my whole spirit rises up against me and tells me it is almost my duty to shirk it, for your sake . . . and yet here I am, pen once more in hand. I do implore you, read it to the very end. I do not say the bitter end. The bitterness comes well before. In this case, the end is all.

Well at least I have happy things to tell you at the start. You must not think all our nights in that Tower of Delight were like my first. Lord, even I would not have survived. Nor – and this will surprise you, I know – nor was our only lover the Comte! He had a wide circle of friends, some cultured, some sporting . . . some even commercial. And, of course, other aristocrats and military by the score. Among them were many who shared his profoundly held views on the beauty and civilizing value of carnal pleasure, and so he shared us with them.

By that I do not mean he *offered* us to them. We were never chattels of his to dispose of at his whim like that. No, it was more subtly done. Among us all it was understood that we girls were, indeed, available to any of his friends who desired us – but we, not they, had the say in the matter. And if we said no, then nothing followed. Naturally, it required a great deal of tact, both in putting forward the suggestion and then in accepting or refusing. And even if one of us had accepted a man last time, a refusal was still possible this. You no doubt think it must have provoked a great deal of awkwardness, but the atmosphere there was so free and easy I do not remember anyone's ever taking offence, either at being asked or refused. And I never knew a man who, having been hot for one of us, and being then refused, did not find solace with another, for our thoughts were so much upon amatory dalliance there it was a wonder that the meanest of them was not showered with grateful acceptances.

But I have not told you who *we* were. It was, of course, a shifting population. Some girls could cope with all that freedom, others could not. But we numbered, in general, ten or a dozen. The Comte, who was as insatiable as any man I ever knew (and still is, bless him), enjoyed each of us at least once a week, when he was in residence – which was over forty weeks out of the fifty-two. Usually singly but often in couples or threes. During my two years among them I suppose I met some twenty girls. Only one of them was of that sort who actually prefers other girls to

108

the solace of a man – Sarah Guilbert. Curiously enough she was even more sought after by the men than the rest of us. (Except, perhaps for me. I have to admit I was always something of a favourite there. For one thing, I never once refused any man . . . but I'll come to that anon.)

Sarah was a marvellous lover of women and on days when we had been lonely we vied with one another for her company overnight. I never knew a girl there sleep alone or one who had to procure her own solo relief. (Talking of which, I used, in the beginning, to ask the Comte to let me have again that wonderful ivory dildo with its little vibrating heart. But he would never comply. He told me its only good purpose was to be used as I had done – in those first discoveries we all must make in the variable erotic powers of our flesh. If we used it thereafter, in our ordinary loving, as a way of multiplying our delight beyond our bodies' unaided capacities, we should soon exhaust all our natural ability and be forced to rely on it ever after. He was such a wise man always – though he lets me use it now, from time to time. As I have managed so magnificently all these years without its artificial aid, there is little fear of my addiction now, he says. Oh, to be sure, a wise man, indeed.) But what was I saying?

Ah yes, I was explaining our system here back in 1816. Have I really lived so long?

Sarah apart, the rest of us would much rather feel the pressure of a man, however clumsy, than the lighter touch of a woman, however skilled. That is the way of things. But also we were young . . . we loved experiment . . . we were all athirst for novelty (else we should hardly have been there in the first place!) . . . so it was only natural we should as often gratify each other as a man – more often, perhaps, when you think how much we were thrown together and how great is a woman's capacity for ecstasy, compared to that of a man.

I cannot mention them all, but there was one with whom I struck up an especial friendship, indeed, we shared a room from the very beginning, though she had been there a month or two before me. She was a black-amoor girl called Nana. The Comte had rescued her on a visit to Morocco, where he had seen her being cruelly abused by her then owner; she was a slave who had been sold into a brothel there. He brought her to us, not really intending for her to join our games but to be a kind of pet sister whom we could slowly initiate into our ways.

Her frame was by nature slight and she had, moreover, been starved and ill-treated to such a degree that, though in her seventeenth year, you would not have put her above fourteen in age. This at first inclined the Comte to leave her untouched for a season, but, by and by the thought of enjoying her was something the Comte could not put out of his mind. He agonized with himself for weeks, and by the time I joined them, he was still in a highly erotic agony of indecision. That was why he put me to share her room. He trusted me to guide his choice.

Well, after three nights with her I had not the slightest doubt that she was ready – at least physically. The abuse she had suffered in that brothel had long since healed, for almost a year had elapsed between her rescue and her coming to France, never mind the month or so that had passed since. But her mind had been damaged by what those brutes had done, and she could never believe that coupling with a man could possibly bring on any pleasure. I tried her myself, and, though her breath grew short and her blood began to race, there was no *great* response within her. And yet, I thought, a man of the Comte's prowess and skill, not to mention his tenderness, which came from his great love of women and his adoration of their flesh . . . I

110

supposed that if anyone could quicken her desires, he would manage it.

I asked if he wished me there too, but he declined the offer – which hurt me, I must confess. However, when he set his mind to a task, or to a pleasure, he never rested until it was done. How I cursed myself for my advice over the weeks that followed – and the other girls cursed me, too. For now our lover's only Love, it seemed was Nana. Night after night she went to him – and came back an hour or so later, brooding and silent. I asked her what had happened but she would only shake her head. The first night, indeed, she came back crying.

Soon I began to think my judgement was the worst on earth. I saw everything through the red-rimmed eyes of my own powerful lusts – which, had it not been for the Comte's wide circle of friends, I would now have had no means of gratifying. At last I felt I should apologize to the Comte for having given him such bad advice.

'Bad advice?' he echoed. 'Dear gazelle! I'd back your judgement now against Solomon's.' Then he added, 'Mind you, after my first encounter with her, I wouldn't have said as much. But now? I don't know where you derive so much wisdom.'

And then I began to notice little changes in Nana's mood. She became happier, more skittish. The Comte would come to fetch her each night in a most peculiar manner – at least, it was quite unlike anything he did with the rest of us. He would wait until we were all fast asleep, sometime around two or three in the morning, and then he'd steal into our room with a small nightlight and gently shake her awake. As soon as her eyes fell open, no matter how blearily, he'd rise and leave us. Not a word was said.

The first night she rose and followed him, her head still bowed down by slumber. Of course that only made

111

me more furious, thinking with what lightsome tread I would obey even that brusque summons! 'Here,' I called after her, 'Aren't you going to lubricate yourself for him?'

She just walked on out and, as I said, came back weeping softly. I thought I then knew why – though I could not imagine our dear, darling Comte abusing her in that way.

Every night, always in the small hours, he would summon her in that fashion. The few occasions following, she refused to lubricate herself again; but she did not return in tears, either. Nor did she seem miserable.

On the fifth or sixth night, when she answered his summons, she turned back from the door and went over to the window where we kept the creams we used for lubrication. And very shyly she rubbed a dab of it in, giving me a mischievous little grin that I took as the height of provocation. For all that, I saw what a longing glance she gave her bed as she passed it on her way out, and I was sure then I had been wrong about her readiness for him – especially when she fell asleep immediately after her return an hour or so later.

The next night she did the same. And the night thereafter she also rubbed a little of it on her breasts as well. In the moonlight I saw how her nipples swelled and glistened at the touch – and at the thoughts that were no doubt going through her mind. And Lord, how I seethed with jealousy! Even so, there was that same longing glance for the warmth and comfort of her solo bed.

After two more nights of that, I could stand it no more. I had to discover what sort of passion they were enjoying together. They were using the Arabian Nights room, which was the Comte's especial favourite. Fortunately, all the floors on that level were of stone, so there was nothing to creak and give me away. I crept up on them, my heart racing and my eyes all agog. Believe me or not – they were playing at cards! And not an intelligent game either.

112

They were playing Snap! And she was giggling with delight very time she scooped the pool. And he just sat there, fondly shaking his head and staring down at her as if he would love her till the end of time.

I could have wept.

Just before they finished – or at least, before their usual time was up – he said softly, 'Are you ready for me tonight?'

'Tomorrow,' she said at once.

'You always say tomorrow.'

'I really mean it this time.'

'Every night you put that cream on your dear little *cutte*, and now you put in on your breasts as well. And yet you always say tomorrow.'

'I promise. I promise. I promise,' she said, making some ritual sort of gesture with both her hands.

I only just got back to bed in time.

'Isn't he the most marvellous lover?' I asked her with a sleepy smile when she returned.

'Mmmm.' She nodded and looked very pensive.

Next night I followed her down again and was just in time to see him breaking out the cards. But she came swiftly to him and put her hand on his arm. He turned and looked down into those huge, dark, unreadable eyes of hers. She nodded and went across to the divan. Such dignity she had, such grace.

He undressed without haste and sat himself down in an armless chair of gilded rosewood with a deep satin cushion beneath him. How well I knew and loved that chair – and what was about to take place upon it!

She rose and walked to him, gently, hesitantly. If anyone deserved the name Little Gazelle it was she; one false move and I'm sure she would have turned and bolted. He put those marvellous hands about her hips and pulled her onto his lap. And there he carried her fingers down between his thighs, where – I could hardly believe it – his tool lay flaccid and soft. How could he do that? He had somehow denied himself his natural erection so that she could have the pleasure of seeing – and feeling – her power over him.

Believe me, Sweet Fanny, until you have seen it for yourself you cannot know how it thrills a woman to watch. A Lady of Pleasure must frequently entertain a Lover who, in truth, leaves her well nigh indifferent as to her own passions. Even so, I have never undressed a man and seen him naked, with his ramrod throbbing fit to break in two with lust for me, without thinking, 'I did that! I feel nothing for this poor creature yet look what even my indifference can do!' (Of course that feeling does not last. When he is rogering away inside me, I cannot help warming a *little*. And when he has spent and is almost broken with his gratitude for the pleasure I have given . . . well, I tell you, the pleasure of that, though not at all erotic, is nonetheless good.)

But again I digress. (I know why, too.) I was telling you I understood the pleasure the Comte knew he was giving Nana by letting her feel her power over him. Then, when he was good and stiff, he let her play with it, and tickle its knob, and grasp it and move her hand up and down – and she saw the effect that had on him, too. In the end he spent into her hand, crying out with delight while she pushed it away and then grasped it . . . and pushed it away . . . not knowing what to do.

I thought that would be it for another night, but Nana had ideas of her own. He, much closer than me, saw that mute pleading of her eyes and acceded to it. Grasping her round her *derrière* he raised her up and, turning her to face him, gently lowered her upon him. From the way he was sitting he would only have three or so inches in her. She arched her back and gave out one long sigh of fulfilment. I don't suppose it was actually a climax – more a little moan of triumph. She had defeated something within herself at last.

He could not resist the temptation to reach forward and suckle her nipples, which were now engorged and huge, like a cow's when the dairymaid has forgotten to milk it. The nerves in that taut skin must have felt half-flayed already, for the slightest touch – and no one could touch more gently than he – made her shiver and cry out in joyful surprise.

How I loved that man then for what he had done!

Why have I gone off at this tangent? It is not what I truly meant to say . . . what I *must* say. I think it is for this reason: I wish you to understand what a truly gentle and sensitive man the Comte is. You will find that hard to believe in what follows; but I have just proved to you that superficial appearances can be the greatest deceivers of all. What was I to make of the brusque and callous way he shook her awake each night? Forcing her to lubricate herself for him and then follow down, like the worst sort of female slave! Well, you see how wrong I was, though I thought I knew him so well. So do not you fall into the same trap, Sweet Fanny, for you do not know him at all.

I told you how we girls were freely available to all his friends, and how I was known never to refuse any request that came my way. It was not simply that I had a capacity for lust no amount of men could satisfy for long; I was also . . . what can I say? Caught up. Trapped in my delight with this new toy. Men were like a new toy to me. A man once told me, quite seriously, he wanted to enjoy every woman in France before he died. He feared I'd think him mad, but I knew precisely what he meant. Do you know what my silliest little daydream was at that time? I was told that the Scottish regiments wear nothing beneath their kilts. Yes! Everything dangles free under there.

Well, I used to lie in bed at night – and this might be on a day when I had been well and truly rogered five or six times, it made no matter – I'd lie in my bed and imagine one of those regiments marching down the street. And I, crafty I, would fall through the ropes in a faint as they passed. And what an eyeful I would get!

Isn't that absurd? I was horn-mad, you see.

After about a year of this, when my passion was abating to a more natural level, as, of course, it had to sooner or later . . . Oh, by the way, after the Comte made little Nana a true Woman, he no longer took her down to the Arabian Nights room for their frolics together. That was when I had my reward! For he came almost nightly to us for several weeks – while still keeping up his obligations of love with the others, mind – and he and Nana and I discovered new delights together on every one of them.

Anyway, after about a year of this, when I thought I had seen it all and done it all and knew it all backwards, the Comte came to me and said, 'What you have experienced here, you know, is only one small part of the pleasures that men and women enjoy together.'

'I cannot imagine anything I have not done,' I laughed.

'No,' he agreed. 'I think it's time you were shown.'

His solemnity filled me with apprehension and I remembered his prediction, back in the days when he first brought me here, that I would one day pass far beyond him. I reminded him of it now and asked him if this was the moment. 'God, I hope not,' he said, 'and yet I cannot deny you the chance to find out for yourself.'

'You mean you won't be coming with me . . . wherever it is I'm supposed to be going?'

'I can't. It's not . . . it's not for me.'

'But why?'

'Don't make me explain it, little gazelle. Some of the things you do now – if I had been foolish enough to explain them to you those first few days in the main guard – you'd have run a thousand miles. And you'd never have known what you'd be missing.'

He was right, of course. He didn't even need to remind me of my disgusted reaction to his assurance that I would soon find almost as much pleasure with women as with men. And what about Love with Miss Brown? I had seen it in his illustrations and thought it utterly disgusting.

Now I began to feel intrigued. What could these new practices be that were beyond even his capacity, but which he could not deny me the chance to try – on the grounds that they might be within mine?

'What if I find I am not up to it?' I asked. 'These new carnal pleasures, whatever they are.'

'You can come straight back here, of course.'

The speed of his answer was most reassuring of all. What could be so awful in at least trying it, I thought, especially as I could break it off at any time and come back. But he corrected me when I said as much. 'No,' he said. 'If you go, it will be for a month, exactly one month.'

'You mean, I'll be a prisoner of some kind?'

He nodded. 'Virtually so. You won't be alone. There'll be several other young ladies there with you.'

'All prisoners, too?'

'No. They are all there voluntarily – for their pleasure. And if you find you like it, you can stay there, too, and become one of them.'

'Am *I* to be their pleasure? Is it that sort of thing?'

'Not at all. In that respect it is the same as here. They are there for the pleasure of men – and the men give them their joy in return.'

'Well then – what can be so bad? Why won't you say?'

But he would not. In the end, of course, I agreed to go. A month! What could happen to me in a month?

The place, he told me, was not too far away. It was owned by a certain Marquis de Q. whose lands marched with his. I and Q.'s other Ladies of Pleasure would not reside in the main château, however, but in a new mansion he had built deep in the woodlands of his demesne. 'You can actually see it from the roof of this tower,' he added – and took me up to prove it.

Then, of course, I felt better still. 'I'll be able to see our Château from there, too, then,' I chortled gaily.

'Yes,' he agreed. 'At least I hope you will.'

The carriage drive took only half an hour. Though it was a fine sunny day we drove in an enclosed brougham with the blinds drawn down. I was dressed in a gorgeous new outfit the Comte had bought for the occasion. I was full of excitement for he had restored to me that sense of trepidation and uncertainty that always does so much to heighten my sensual pleasure. He, however, remained calm and remote – a little sad, even, which both touched and flattered me. When we were nearly there he said, 'You know you have never refused one of my friends your favours?'

'Of course I know.' I laughed.

'Even though no one would have thought the worse of you for it.'

I shrugged.

'Why?' he asked.

'I don't know. I just felt so thirsty for experience. How do I know the man I refused wasn't the one to give it me?'

He smiled and patted my thigh. 'That's good. You really are quite splendid, little gazelle. Just recall that answer when you're with Q. I mean – if you find it not . . . not really to your liking.'

When we drew up he suddenly remembered one thing more. 'What are you wearing under that dress?' he asked, almost in alarm.

118

'Petticoats . . .'

'No, no – next to your *cutte*?'

'My drawers – as usual. Why?'

'Take them off!'

'What – here?'

'Yes – at once. And never wear anything like that in there. All the women in there go naked beneath their skirts.'

And he threw up my gorgeous dress and my acres of creamy petticoats and almost ripped off the offending garment. The sight of me down there – perhaps for the last time in his life – was too much for him and he burst into tears.

Ten minutes later, as his coach drew away, I covered the last remaining steps to the door of my new home, still breathless from the wonderful rogering he had just given me, and feeling his milt running down my now naked thighs.

I raised my hand to the great brass door knocker, which was in the form of a huntsman's riding crop . . .

No, I cannot go on. I'll tell you another time.

Frances
Comtesse de C.

LETTER NINE

FROM MOUNT VENUS,
Monday, 22nd April, 1850

*[There was no opening salutation to this letter;
it plunged directly into its narrative.]*

'How *dare* you?'

'What?' I asked, all bewildered, for the grim portals of the Maison Q. had only just closed behind me.

'How dare you look me in the eyes?' And he dealt me a stinging slap across my face.

I think I was too startled even to cry out. I raised my hand to my cheek and rubbed it tenderly.

'You are *still* doing it,' he yelled in a fury and, quick as lightning, slapped me on the other cheek even harder.

I burst into tears.

'That's better,' he said. 'What are you wearing under that tawdry dress?'

I just buried my face in my hands and went on weeping.

'As you love your skin you'd better answer.' His voice was filled with a dreadful menace and I felt him grasp me by the elbow. His strong, sinewy fingers found some special nerve such that, when he pressed me there, the pain that shot up and down my arm was unbearable.

'Nothing!' I cried out.

'Show me. And remember – do not look me in the eye.'

Slowly I lifted my skirts for his inspection; for the first time in my sensual life I felt something unclean in the action.

'Turn round,' he snapped.

I obeyed.

'And when I ask a thing like that I expect you to know what I mean. Get those skirts up again!'

Sullenly I obeyed.

'Not bad!' he said in an admiring tone, running his hands softly over my little *derrière*.

How pathetic and abject I had already become! I almost wept again, for joy this time, to hear that gentleness in him. *Come now*, I thought to myself. *This is not so bad. Little Miss Laycock can subdue all to her ways in the end.* I felt his fingers go inside me. Then he withdrew them and sniffed.

'Milt!' he cried. 'God but these lips have seen some traffic to judge by their looks. You're a whore.'

'I am not!' I cried stoutly.

I felt a vicious slap on that other cheek, down there – but why, I wondered was I still bending over, exposing myself like that?

'Never, never contradict a Master,' he said. This time

122

there was no anger in his tone; the words came more as advice than anything.

'I am not a whore,' I insisted, beginning to rise.

'Who told you you may do that?' he barked.

Meekly I returned to that position of subservience. Oh, Sweet Fanny, I obeyed! Even then I could hardly believe it. Where had my spirit fled?

He slapped me once more, the hardest of all; and I just stood there, motionless, my breath heaving, and I said nothing.

'That's better,' he said after a moment's silence.

He got out his tool and pushed it hard into me. It was about the same length as Love Lane but in that position he could ram against the *cul de sac* of her. I gave a little moan and tensed my buttocks, as if of pleasure, and that prevented him from going to the hilt a second time. Now he grabbed my hips and started rogering away in earnest. And I'll tell you a most extraordinary thing, my dear, but the places where he had slapped me – on my *derrière*, I mean – were now glowing like mad. And the feeling had turned to pleasure! I will not say it was the most intense pleasure I had ever felt (as I'm sure you'll believe by now!), but that, coupled with his engine, rogering away inside me, brought me very near to an ecstasy on the spot.

I felt his excitement rising, too, but the moment before he got there, he withdrew and, turning on his heel, walked away down the corridor.

'I'm not going to stay here,' I called after him.

He spun round and came a few paces back. 'You are. You've made a contract.'

'I signed nothing.' How I wished I could look at his face, but already I did not dare risk it. I had gained only the most confusing glimpse in those first bewildering moments; all I could remember now were his dark,

123

hypnotic eyes, deep set beneath his craggy brows. He would have been about fifty, I guessed.

'We'll sign it now, if you like,' he sneered. 'In blood!'

I ran to the door but found it had somehow locked itself. I turned the key . . . and turned it and turned it . . . He laughed. 'Try the windows next, whore!'

I almost refused. But then I saw that might be his purpose, so I raced into the first room that led off the entrance hall and dashed straight to the nearest window. They were tall and elegant – and secured in the easiest manner of all, by espagnolet bolts. But they were fakes. Try as I might, they would not turn; and when I inspected them more closely, I saw they were all one casting. In fact, as I later learned, every window in the Maison Q. was a single, rigid casting of bronze and quite incapable of opening.

I half-collapsed, laying my forehead against the thick plate glass and stared out into a sylvan glade, a wide, park-like clearing in a forest of magnificent chestnut trees. Little fawns that had been startled by the approach of the Comte's brougham were now coming shyly out to graze again. Little gazelles! I thought of the way *he* always said it and then broke down in tears of abject bitterness.

Moments later I felt a gentle touch at my elbow and a voice, a woman's, said, 'That was very good!'

Startled, I turned to face her – or them, as I now discovered. They must have been in that room all along; perhaps they had seen what had just passed between that ogre and me – they must certainly have overheard it, anyway. There were two of them, both dressed in a style I can only describe as Puritan – grey, drab cloth buttoned right up to their throats, and skirts that fell all the way to the ground without padding or underskirts of any kind. They wore no make-up. Nor did I in those days, mind,

124

but my skin did not have that ghostly pallor, nor was there that strange haunted look in *my* eyes.

'Good?' I echoed, thinking it the last word I would choose.

'You are the new serf-girl,' said my interlocutrice.

(I must explain. The French word she used was *serve*, which was a coinage of their own, for the proper word, as I'm sure you know, is *serf*, which can only be masculine in gender. And in *that* house, everything that was masculine – in gender, if not in humanitarian character – was called Maître – Master!)

'What is your name?' she continued.

'Fanny,' I told them.

'That is what *we* will call you,' said the other. 'I am Alice. *They* call me Scribbler.'

'And I,' said the other, 'am Charlotte. *They* call me Slut. Come, let us find you a more fitting costume. *They* do not like to be provoked by such finery as this.'

'Who are they?' I asked as they led me out into the hall and up the stairs.

'Our Masters,' Alice said admiringly.

'And who was that monster who greeted me in that way?'

They laughed. 'Didn't you know? That was the Marquis de Q. himself!'

'It was a great honour,' Alice assured me. 'Your reputation, whatever it may be, has gone before you.'

'Did you realize he very nearly spent inside you?' Charlotte asked, with an odd sort of sigh – as if to imply she would never be so lucky.

'Yes – why didn't he finish?' I asked.

That only made them laugh the louder.

They took me to a grand chamber that led off the upper landing. Everything was done out in the most sumptuous taste – overdone, to my way of thinking.

125

Gold leaf and red plush and buhl and ormulu and ivory-decorated *chinoiserie* and inlaid floors with Turkey rugs as soft as mattresses and I don't know what else. It contrasted most strongly with the utterly drab clothing we females were required to wear – but that, to be sure, was the purpose.

As I shed each garment, they took it and folded it carefully, stroking its rich decoration with a loving sort of wistfulness. I had to take off everything, even my chemise, which was of silk and felt so lovely when it clung to my skin. Alice looked me up and down admiringly. 'Oh, you'll please *them*,' she said with great assurance.

Charlotte touched the bright red handmarks on my *derrière* and tried to fit her own to their shape. There was something deeply loving in the action, but it was not love of me.

They took me to a bath – stone cold, of course, but it was summer, so not too disagreeable. 'We have to remove every last trace of perfume,' they explained. Then they dried me in a towel of the coarsest material I had ever felt – until, that is, they brought out my new dress. It was composed of two layers. The outer one – the one that faced the world (and our Masters) – was, as I said, drab in colour and design, but smooth and soft in texture. But the inner one! Well, I would not have made hopsacks from that cloth! And that was what I was supposed to wear next my skin.

I refused at once, of course.

'But it's what we all wear,' Alice assured me. And they turned up their own dresses to prove it; and indeed it was true.

'But it must scratch you to death!'

Charlotte closed her eyes and said, 'Mmmm!'

As they dressed me and combed out my hair, before tying it into the plainest sort of bun, they explained some of the rules of the House. 'And these,' they said, 'will apply just as much when you graduate from being a serf-girl and join us Slaves.'

'You never look a Master in the face unless he specifically commands it.'

'You never wear anything between this dress and your body.'

Alice picked up a little bottle of oil – olive oil, as I later learned. She showed it me and then popped it in the pocket that normally holds the fobwatch. 'You will always carry this lubrication with you, for every hole in your body is available to any Master you may meet, at any time, day or night. He will tell you if he wishes to avail himself of it.'

Charlotte thought this required a little expansion. 'When you run across a Master, anywhere, you turn away from him and bow your head. But in a corridor or on the stair you face the wall and flatten yourself against it until he is well past. If he wishes to use you, he will give you his commands . . .'

'. . . which,' Alice added, 'you will obey at once and without question . . .'

'. . . no matter how bizarre or obscene they may be,' Charlotte concluded with that same wistful sigh.

I stared at them in horror. I had obviously fallen into some kind of asylum – a Bedlam for people whose lunacy centred on their sexual being! Everything I had discovered since meeting the Comte – all that was most sublime and tender and joyous to me – was here to be made drab, foul, disgusting, joy*less*.

A month! How could I endure it so long? No no, I must get away – the Comte must be told about his appalling neighbour. He obviously had no idea what was going on here; he probably thought it no more than a romping, joyous sort of spanking – which, come to think of it,

Sweet Fanny, our darling namesake of the last century, Fanny Hill, found she quite relished – as long as it were not overdone.

The two willing Slaves saw my consternation. 'But isn't this what you have chosen?' Alice asked.

I shook my head vehemently – and now the consternation was theirs.

We went downstairs and joined the sorority of Slaves. We were eight in all, including me, but I shall not bother to introduce you all round just now. You shall meet most of them anon. What a serious lot they were – quite unlike the happy band of voluptuous hoydens I had left behind me. Two of them, Hortense and Annette (*grandes dames* to me – well up in their thirties) were actually corresponding members of the *Académie des Arts et des Sciences!* They had devoted most of their lives to the collection and classification of the flora and insects of our part of France; specimens arrived in almost every post and they worked most of the day in the huge library on the ground floor. *They* called them Bug and Weed.

There was something of that sort about all of them. Alice (Scribbler) had had several volumes of poetry published – beautiful verse it was, too. (I anticipate my story here, for I had many conversations with her over the following weeks and in the end had read everything she wrote.) Charlotte (Slut) was a superb needlewoman, and was devoting her days to the repair of the tapestries from the Château – which, as you may not know, for who does such work nowadays?, requires the very highest skills.

And so on. Briefly, Millie (Farter) was a consummate horsewoman and had schooled the Marquis's horses to the point where his stables had become the Mecca for horsemen all over France. Gudrun (Hag) was the prettiest young girl I had seen in years – a Dane with unruly hair that always got her into trouble. (She later confessed to me, as if it were the naughtiest thing ever and please don't tell *Them*, that the word *hag* in Danish means charm!) She could dash off a water colour like nobody else; the Marquis's friends all vied to buy them from her. Fleur (Stink) was a slight exception; she sat around all day reading lecherous novels and trying to get the rest of us to sneak off to some quiet corner with her for some fun together. But when she set her mind to it she could go down into the kitchens, take full charge of everything – even M. Maurice, who was a proud and temperamental old devil – and turn out a banquet that the whole province would be talking about for months.

Well there now, I *have* introduced them all, Sweet Fanny. I do not wish to devote much time to this particular Lesson in my sentimental education, but now that I have forced myself to it, I find it hard to relinquish. I feel I still have not drawn from it all the . . . wisdom? No. All the . . . *understanding* I might have gained. I wilfully shut my mind to it at the time, and I have not cared (or do I mean dared?) to open it since. Anyway . . .

'And what do *you* do, my dear?' they asked with interest.

What did I do? I craved the company of lusting men. I longed to see how their desire rose to fever pitch all because of my charms. I loved to provoke them to take my longings up there with them. I itched to be free of our clothes and go bang together as randy old Mother Nature intended. That was me! I spent most of my hours in a kind of melting, jolly dream of knobs and *cuttes* and breasts and *derrières* and skilled fingers . . . oh, and silks and perfumes and spices and wines . . .

I was, in short, a Slave! Yes, I was as much a slave to my Joyous God Eros as were these sad ladies to their own dark Devil, whose hundred names I still cannot say. But what did I *do*?

'Oh, I write a little, you know,' I said airily.

'But you are so young!'

'Yes, I know. I've had nothing published yet, of course . . .'

Well, now that I have o'ershot so much of my tale – for I did not discover all these matters slap-bang that first afternoon, of course – I must set it in context before I return to what happened that evening, which really was the most extraordinary thing. These Slaves enjoyed that title (and I do not speak in irony now), they *enjoyed* that title and office only in relation to their passionate natures. If you think of it, it must be so – for if they were abject slaves in all departments of their lives, they would be as worms. Nothings. Nobodies. And who would then think it worth taking one step aside to crush them? Why he would but demean himself who did it.

No, the more eminent or skilled the Slave – the more prominent she was in the esteem of the world – then the greater the Master's pleasure in abusing her, abasing her, making her feel like the worm she *wasn't*! There now – is that not a pretty paradox! But why did they tolerate it, you may ask? Even now I cannot really answer you. It was the one question I asked myself, and them, again and again, during my time in that place. It was the strangest thing to see the Marquis or one of his friends, deep in the most earnest conversation about some abstruse point of philosophy and literature – with Alice, for instance – talking face to face like two equals, and she giving him as good as she got, and he taking it and coming back with yet another fine point . . . and then suddenly, with both in full and equal flight, he would slap her face for no reason at all, or command her to bend over and draw up her skirts while he . . . I will not say 'rogered', it is too sweet a word to me – I will break a rule and use a whore's word for it . . . while he *screwed* away without a scrap of

130

tenderness or affection for her at all. And he would never spend in her, either, nor in any Slave; for he believed it would rob him of his power. Yet she would just lie there and moan in pleasure at it! And all the while he watched to see when she would rise to her climax, and then, when she was poised on her very threshold, he would withdraw and leave her, unfilled and unfulfilled. But that, to her, was the sweetest thing of all! I said 'twas one great Paradox – that thwarting of her lust would then brim her over *in solo*, and she would lie there gasping and panting as I have heard myself go so many times, but always with a man to plug the Hole of Joy.

I say this would happen with Alice – it was the same with them all. Ladies of taste, refinement, learning, and achievement – all. Their greatest pleasure was to abase themselves in that way. Why did they not choose stable boys and scullions? Surely that would make their abasement the greater? But no, 'twas the same argument, you see. To be abased by one who knew no better, who thought mere *screwing* the very height of human Pleasure – where was the value in that? But when 'twas done by a man like the Marquis, who could talk art and literature and statesmanship with the finest in the land . . . when great nobleman stoops to degradation, why then 'twas very *bliss* for them!

Now here's a difficult thing for me to confess. As these truths broke over me – listening to their conversation and watching them at work and 'play' – as I began to learn I had not, after all, strayed into some Bedlam for the sexually insane – I made no very deep question of those *women's* motives. Now wasn't that an awful thing? Somewhere inside me, you see, I could *almost* understand them. Even then I had tasted enough of Love's infinite variety to know that somewhere within me was a Seat of Pleasure that loved to be told by a lover, not harshly, mind, but with a definite voice of command: 'Do this . . . turn that way . . . lie so . . . spread your thighs . . . wider . . .' and so on. It is the verbal equivalent of that more physical Thrill I always feel when a powerful man puts both hands round my hips or *derrière* and moves me or shakes me as he wishes. I melt and lose all power to resist them, even in play.

Now that, I think, is the very smallest beginning of the Pleasure these women found in their chosen Slavery. If I am right, then I believe there is something of that choice *waiting to be made* in all us poor Females. Perhaps it is old Eros's way of balancing things out. For the enormous Capacity for Voluptuousness which He has allowed us Women, when contrasted with the single shot most Men carry in their lockers, would make us Absolute Sovereigns of the Kingdom of Love. True, we are pretty nearly that as it is. We can pick and choose as we wish – *and* be well rewarded for it in both Ecstasy and gold – but our sovereignty there is not Absolute. We all nurse that little worm of abasement, ready to gnaw our giblets out; and in these Slaves it had gorged itself into a Mighty Serpent. So I did not question these females' purposes too searchingly, fearing to discover I was closer to them beneath the skin than I'd willingly claim!

What I questioned instead was the purposes of the *Men* – the Masters as they boasted themselves to be. The only man I had ever known to compare to them was that loathsome old verger, Dan King, who caught me and sweet young H-day, the curate, behind the altar in the Lady Chapel. All I did was fondle his tool a little – the curate's, I mean – just out of curiosity, really, for I had only the haziest notions then of the true Joys of Venery. I did not know the lad had 'a shaved trigger' and would spend in such a flood all over the place, including me. And then, when Dan King came to me after and suggested

132

all manner of disgusting things we might do together (though I would do them all gladly now with most other men – I only say they were disgusting to me *then*), what could I do but run away? (I left him in a good old fix, though! I wrote a note to my mother, naming him and setting forth those same disgusting things as if they had been accomplished fact and said I could no more look Decent Society in the face and was gone off to earn my living in what way I could. On the strength of that letter, Dan King was transported to Van Diemen's Land – and was lucky to escape hanging, I think.) Anyway, he was the only man I could compare these Masters to in their treatment of Women. Yet they were men, as I say, of the utmost taste and civilization while he was little above the brutes. And that question – why are these Masters as they are? – perplexed me far more than the same question concerning their Slaves.

I was no wiser that evening, though I had a great opportunity to see them in action.

It was the custom of the Maison Q. to dine at six. A little before that hour we changed into our 'evening gowns'. These were soft, light garments of silk, similar above the waist to the ones Elaine, Garence, and I had worn in the Arabian Nights room that night – oh, how long ago it now seemed! But the frills were more numerous, so that a deliberate movement had to be made of it if *They* wished (or we were obliged) to bare our breasts. Below the waist it was not the cut of the hem that was revealing but the way it clung to our naked bodies just beneath, for we never wore drawers or chemises nor anything that would hamper a Master's ability to get at us. From the lie of the silk you could see our navels, the clefts of our *derrières*, the fold below ... almost everything; and yet the material was so elastic it could be whipped up in a flash. And around our waists we each wore a light

133

chain of gold with a curiously large clip, with a spring – like those that hold bundles of paper together – two clips, in fact, one in front and one behind. The purpose of these, Alice told me, was that if a Master commanded it, we were to roll up our dresses, in front or behind, or both, and secure them by these clips; thus they could get at us in either way – 'or both,' she added, 'if there are two of *Them*.'

She spoke in a kind of dreamy indulgence. Indeed, all of them (for we changed in one common dressing room) seemed filled with an excited . . . dreaminess – there is no other word for it. They moved slowly, gracefully, and stared at each other and me through half-closed eyes, and they wore a permanent sort of half-smile, with their lips opened in a way that suggested all kinds of lascivious things – or would have done if this were my own dear Comte's Château. Here, I could not imagine *what* it might portend.

We went down and joined our Masters in a happy, laughing throng – believe it if you will. And they received us in every way as gentlemen should, with gallantry, flattery, courtesy, and charm. I understood there was a general amnesty or permission to look *Them* in the face at this time. (Again, if the interdiction were permanent, where would be its force? The entire Rule of the Maison Q. was founded in the unexpected. At any moment, the sun could go in and storm and lightning and thunder would rage. You never knew when that fury would descend about you. And I have to confess it gave an edge of excitement to Life that was insidiously Pleasant at times – but I shall come to that anon.)

I took full advantage of this amnesty to look at my Marquis at last; and I had every chance to do so since I was seated as guest of honour at his right. In his present mood I found him charming and handsome – and much younger than I had taken him to be in that first violent encounter. In fact, he was little over thirty and, in my view, the very best age for a Lover, since a man of that decade in his life still has the stamina of youth but has added to it by then the wiles of amorous experience. I began to have hopes of him.

'And what have you learned today, my dear?' he asked me kindly.

I told him as best I could; it was my first, hesitant attempt to outline the thoughts I have given you above. But he understood me exactly; he had that sharp sort of mind that can always go to the heart of any matter.

'You know you are something of an experiment for us,' he said.

I asked how he might mean that.

'All these other Slaves, when they first came here as Serf-girls, already knew what sort of Rule we follow; they chose to come here – quite voluntarily – knowing what would be expected of them. But you, I understand, are here out of curiosity alone.'

'I hope it is a little more than mere curiosity, sir,' I countered.

He smiled – and in that smile I caught a flash of that cruelty I had glimpsed before. 'Yes,' he echoed, 'so do we all.' He became genial once again. 'It could be highly dangerous to us, you know.'

I laughed. 'Oh, I hardly think that, sir.'

But he was not jesting. 'But of course you could. We feed each other here on pure Illusion. Our meat and drink is Paradox.'

I frowned, having no idea what he might mean.

'Surely?' he urged. 'Is there not a similar illusion, mademoiselle, an identical paradox, at the centre of all voluptuary pleasures?'

'How could I know that, sir? I have no experience beyond the Château C.'

'And you do not consider *that* an illusion? Is it not founded on the dream of that man's tireless priapism and his hareem of infinitely libidinous girls? Isn't that why you've come here – looking for something more?'

'But M. le Comte *can* roger away all night,' I assured him. 'And as for our infinite lib-libidinity – whatever it is . . .'

'Libido,' he offered with a superior smile.

I have never liked those courtroom words: libido, *membrum virile*, the Act of Kind . . . and so on. I only ever hear them used by dry impotent old sticks who have forgotten what it is they're trying to talk about. 'As for our Capacity for Ecstasy,' I said coolly, 'I can speak most surely for myself. And I can assure you I have had as profound a climax at dawn with him as at dusk the night before – and a dozen or more between. Many and many a time.'

His eyes shone at this. I thought I was getting him roused. But in fact, he saw me only as a challenge – as I was very soon to discover.

All during the meal, though our conversation was as civilized as ever, I became aware that that dreamy sort of electricity among the Slaves, that feeling of a mighty thunderstorm brewing in their emotions, was about to erupt. It came as soon as the meal was over.

'Punishments!' cried the Marquis.

A silence such as I have rarely heard fell at once; it was that hush you get among a crowd at a hanging, when the poor wretch on the gallows is about to be sent off into eternity. You know how everyone stops breathing at that moment? Well, it was like that.

The servants had already cleared the table and gone; we were left alone with our revels.

'Scribbler!' the Marquis barked.

Alice rose, pale and shivering – and yet with that

strange smile still on her lips. 'Master?' she replied, looking down at his feet.

'Confess.'

She began a recital, almost a chant: 'First, I failed to
give Master S. true pleasure this morning. Second, I did
not abase myself swiftly enough . . .' Her voice trembled
and failed as it does in inexperienced public speakers at
times; but she recovered swiftly and went on: '. . . to abase
myself before you, my Master of Masters. And I now
freely and voluntarily add this to my offences – thirdly,
that I had lascivious thoughts, without the permission of
any Master, about our new Serf-girl.'

She did not look at me. No one looked at me.

'And her name is?'

'Whore.'

The Marquis turned to me, daring me to deny it. I
stared him out.

'I'll come to you,' he promised me quietly. Then, turning back to poor Alice, he said, 'Three.'

I thought it was the tally of her offences but it was, in
fact, the sentence. Three Masters rose to their feet – they
went in rank from the head of the table. The most senior
approached Alice from behind and said, 'Up!'

She lowered herself as if in a curtsey until her skirt
spread out over the floor. She felt for the back seam and,
by long experience, I suppose, began to roll the hem at
that point toward her. Then she stood and completed the
action, bringing the roll of it right up to the gold band
that circled her waist. There she clipped it. Her hands
were trembling violently by now and she could barely
manage it; but no one moved to assist her. The three
Masters were staring in delight at her now naked . . . no,
I will not call it *derrière*. That is an organ of pleasure to
me, which had no part in these proceedings. They stared
in delight at her naked buttocks – there! The other

Slaves were watching in a kind of . . . I can only call it rapture.

The three Masters took her gently by the elbows and guided her toward an elegant Chinese screen that stood some three feet away from the wall. I had taken it to be the place of ease, since few houses at that time, either in England or France (and certainly not France!) had proper water closets, or even earth closets, either. Indeed, I had seen the Slaves glancing toward it from time to time during our meal and I had supposed they needed some special consent to go and make use of it.

Now two of the Masters folded it up and laid it to one side. No little throne and chamberpot was revealed, however. Instead there was an occasional table covered with . . . well, before I had time to take it all in, everyone stood up and moved into a line on the farther side of the table from Alice and her Masters. The Marquis took me by the arm and guided me around there, too. 'Up!' he whispered in my ear, touching my buttocks as he spoke.

It took a moment for the command to register. He had to repeat it: 'Up!' This time it was no whisper, and he added, 'Oh we must teach you to obey quicker than that!'

I curtseyed as Alice had done, but made a poorer job of rolling up my hem. Angrily he told Fleur to redo it for me and put it in the clip.

But then, in that mercurial way of his, which could turn terror to relief, and back to terror again in moments, he put his hand on my nakedness and began to caress me there. It did not rouse me at all, though I thought it best to pretend to some slight, reluctant feeling in that direction. It seemed to satisfy him, anyway. 'Now watch and I will explain,' he murmured, in the kindliest tone, in my ear.

The senior Master had meanwhile blindfolded Alice.

138

The other two had wrapped a golden chain about her wrists – in front of her, not behind – and secured it there with a golden shackle and bolt. One of them now uncoiled a rope from a cleat on the wall. This wall had been at my back during the meal, so all these arrangements were a surprise to me. The rope went up over a strong pulley in the ceiling, with a vicious looking hook at its end. As the rope was payed out, this hook descended, hitting Alice quite a sharp knock on the head. They must have seen it was about to happen but no one made a move to warn her. She gave a little cry of pain and jerked her head back. The hook stopped when it was level with her shoulders. They raised her bound wrists and slipped it through a link of the chain. The senior Master gave a nod and the other two hauled slowly but strongly on the line.

Alice's arms went up as if in prayer. And then on, and on . . . until she gave out a cry of pain. I wondered why she had not made it sooner, for now she could only be comfortable by standing on tiptoe – which she could not do for long. She was thus always caught between one kind of discomfort and another.

And then, to my horror, the three Masters went to the table, which was now out of sight of me, beyond Alice, and selected a cane, a riding crop, and a stout, leather-covered stick. I was still in that state of *Fanny Hill* innocence where I had imagined they were going to spank her with their hands – as the Marquis had done with me that afternoon!

'No!' I exclaimed.

Everyone turned and looked at me the way they would at an interrupter in church.

The Marquis chuckled into my ear. '*You* are the one who's lacking here, my dear,' he said gently. 'Forget your silly prejudices and try to learn.'

I shook my head.

139

'You say your libido ... sorry, your capacity for voluptuary delight – you say it's huge as high Olympus. Easy words, my love! Now prove it. Is it great enough for this? For what you are about to see is the very pinnacle of erotic pleasure – measured against which your nights with the Comte were but the antics of the stud farm.'

Erotic pleasure! I thought but I gave him no answer.

Each Master, as he selected his implement, held it up for the Marquis's approval. The stout, leather-covered stick was turned down in favour of a fresh-cut hazel switch. 'Let's be merciful,' he whispered to me, almost as if the decision were really mine. His exploring hand went down the cleft of my *derrière* – yes, I call it that now because I cannot deny it gave me a *frisson* of pleasure – and started to explore Miss Laycock's little folds and frills. His fingers were as gentle and skilled as his tool had been brusque and harsh. And I could not help myself.

'How can you!' I screamed silently – inside me, yelling at my own body. 'I hate this man! He has not one thing about him I might admire, neither in body nor in mind. And there *you* are, melting away at his touch like that!' Truly, I began to feel an entirely new kind of terror to see myself being carried away so easily.

He was aware of it, too, for he went on working away at me like that – and all the while pouring his insidious beliefs into my ear. I just stood there, straining every nerve to stop myself responding – which is easier said than done. You can tell your muscles to hold still, and they will probably obey; but how do you stop your juices flowing? He soon had me so wet he was able to lubricate me all over down there – half-way down my thighs and up inside Miss Brown as well.

The Masters swished their implements viciously against the air, making them whistle with the most malevolent urgency; but they seemed in no hurry to begin. Poor Alice, blindfolded as she was, could not tell that, of course. She flinched and winced at every sound. She was up on her toes, which tensed the muscles of her buttocks until they quivered, and then down on her heels, wrenching her arms almost out of their sockets. This way and that she squirmed.

'See how she tries to ease herself?' the Marquis murmured. 'She will now accept a greater pain in one arm in order to favour the other. And all the while she's wondering when that first sharp sting will fall. Who will do it? She knows all these Masters. She's been ravished by them all – given them such voluptuous delight, too. Won't they please remember it now, she's wondering. Won't they look down in their lust on that sweet little bottom of hers and recall those moments of utter rapture – and so just give her a gentle tickling? Just enough to warm her and get her a little randy again? She'd love that, but she's not sure she can stand that awful pain again. Her skin can just about remember the last time . . .'

Alice had obviously decided she'd waited long enough. Her breast was heaving as if she'd run a fast mile. She went as high as she could on tiptoe and then, arching her back until I thought it must surely break, she thrust out her tense little buttocks in an invitation that – had those three brutes been half-way normal – not one of them could have resisted. Why, we could even see the lips of her *cutte*, red and engorged and open . . . she was as wet as me down there.

Of course to them it was an invitation of a different kind. The senior Master brought down his riding crop in one short, vicious arc. The smack of it upon her flesh was piteous to me. But my Marquis was ready this time and the cry that rose to my lips was stifled by the flat of his hand – his free hand, that is, for the other was still at its gentle work below. When he was sure I'd make no sound, his hand fell – but only as far as my breasts. There his thumb and fingers slipped in among all the frills and found my nipples already hard as brass. When they began their work, I was undone entirely.

Thwack! Thwack! Down went the hazel switch, down went the cane – an inch above and an inch below the ugly red weal the senior Master had left. And so, while I stood there and shuddered through the most miserable Ecstasy I have ever endured, there was an infinity of pauses and blows, all falling with that same dismaying accuracy on flesh that seemed to know no other trick than to offer itself for yet more punishment. For during all that time Alice uttered nothing more than a deep guttural cry that was both pain and rapture in one.

And the others looked on, not in a trance but entranced.

'Enough,' the Marquis cried at last, releasing me from his touch. 'Let us not forget our sweet young novice. This night belongs to her!'

But for that promise, I think, there would have been a cry of disappointment – and I cannot swear that Alice herself would not have joined it.

'What of me, Master?' called Fleur. 'I am to be punished, too.'

'Oh,' he said casually, 'We can't be bothered to flog you tonight. The steward can do it in your cell.'

'Flog me double tomorrow night . . . please?' she begged. 'Not the steward!'

What a monster that steward must be, I thought, if the threat of him is worse than double this!

'The steward,' he told her firmly. 'And double from him for daring to question your Master of Masters.' Then he turned to me.

And so did all the Slaves; they crowded around me as, in later years, I have seen Ladies of Pleasure crowd around

142

a true virgin about to go to her first Lover – with a strange mixture of sympathy and shared delight.

Fanny, dear – I now wish, more than at any other time in this correspondence, to lay down my pen and cease this tale. But I know that if I do, I shall never take it up again. I know this epistle is already over-long, I know its contents are sickening beyond belief, but can you bear a little more? I think when I have got it out I shall have laid a ghost that has haunted me these three dozen years now gone – a ghost of me, or a me-that-might-have-been. I feel her ahead of me there, somewhere on the still-blank pages that lie beneath this, longing for her exeat. Bear with me then. 'Tis a service I have owed too long.

There was, indeed, almost a mutiny among the Slaves when the Marquis spoke next. His speech was but a single word: 'Out!' But into it he managed to put all his contempt for them, all his authority, all his venom. For a moment they swayed, surging toward him, but his eyes held them and then they were backing down, turning, shuffling disconsolately toward the door – leaving me alone, and, though clothed (after a fashion), feeling more naked and defenceless than at any time in my life. Alone among seven Masters.

'Why?' I whispered, not really to him. My throat was dry as sand.

But he answered me. 'As I said. You are dangerous here. No one knows how you'll stand up to it.'

My stomach seemed to be falling endlessly and I had to fight for my breath. 'What are you going to do to me?' I managed to ask.

'Teach you.'

I looked at the empty hook, now hanging freely from the ceiling.

'Not in here,' he added. 'This is just for ordinary work.'

143

One of his friends opened a door to the room beyond and beckoned me through with a curt flick of his head. It was a drawing room of that comfortable kind you see in gentlemen's clubs – deep leather chairs, thick rugs on polished floors, a sideboard furnished with cigars, port, brandy, and so on, and a cheerful fire.

Though it was summer I was glad of that fire for I now felt miserably chill and shivery. I was even more glad of it a moment later when I heard the Marquis ask his friends, behind me, 'Have her naked, I think?'

'Or we could start as she is. Then lift her front as well. And then strip her,' said another.

'Depends how far we're going to go,' said a third.

'Yes,' the Marquis agreed. 'That's another thing we should settle first – the strategy of the thing. Do we break her slowly over several days, or take her to the limit all at once . . . get it over and done with?'

I just stood there, listening in disbelief to this conversation at my back, and staring into the flames. I was quite sure I was going to die – not that they would deliberately kill me but that my heart would suddenly fail. Already I could feel it labouring, fluttering erratically, giving two beats and then none . . . and then a mighty thump – going all over the place.

'Naked,' the Marquis said decisively. 'We'll have her naked from the start. Then we'll just see how it goes. I suspect she'll be able to stand up to quite a bit.' He raised his voice and called out to me, 'Dear young mademoiselle! Please be so kind as to slip out of your gown. Fold it up with care and place it on one of the chairs.'

Why did I obey? If I had simply turned and walked out of that room, what could they really have done? Even then, as I stood there in the starkest terror I had ever felt, I knew in my bones that they were not interested in hurting just any young woman. The pain was – in an odd sort of way – incidental; what was important was a kind of pact between the giver and the receiver. The woman might be ninety-nine per cent unwilling, ninety-nine per cent hating them and everything they did – but if there was one tiny fragment of her that responded, that was willing to submit, then *that* was what they played on. For it alone made the whole paradox work. Pain, by definition, cannot be pleasure. But if that little golden seed of response is there in the woman, it is enough to make the paradox work. And therein lies their pleasure – hers and theirs – in seeing the impossible come to pass before their eyes.

I think I realized, too – but not in actual words – that this challenge to me came not from them but from my own darling Comte. I have never spoken of it to him . . . never needed to. The profundity of our love makes it unnecessary. But in some way he had said to me I must take this chance, while I was still young and not yet confirmed in my prejudices. I must seize this opportunity of discovering a possible truth about myself – whether that little golden seed lay within me, and whether I wanted to crush it or let it germinate and grow.

I think it must have been some dim realization of that kind which enabled me to comply with the Marquis's request without further ado. I was still terrified, of course. I only needed to look down at my own skin, so pale and goosefleshed to know that. But I no longer thought I might die. I just prayed for strength to endure whatever it was they intended.

The Marquis's arm went round my waist. 'Come and stand by the fire, little dove,' he said. 'You look so cold.' Over his shoulder he called, 'Gentlemen! I leave the choice of instruments to your discretion.'

When we were standing side by side, staring down into that lovely warm blaze, he began to talk to me in a voice that was loving and strong. 'If you had come here as our other serf-girls, I should hardly need to tell you this. You must not think of any Master here as your enemy. They love you already. You are very precious to them all – and even more to me. I confess it – this unease I feel – you have moved me strangely. I thought I had mastered every challenge that could possibly interest me in the whole world of female flesh . . .' I heard him swallow. Then he stood silent awhile.

'How much do you intend to hurt me?' I asked.

It took him some time to collect his answer. I don't think he had worked out anything; this was, as he said, something beyond his ken. '*I* shall not hurt you at all, little petal. I shall be with you throughout.'

'At my side, you mean?'

He caressed my hip and there was a smile in his reply. 'At your front, actually. Come, let's begin. You seem warmer now. Do you want to stand there and take it, or would you rather be chained?'

I just shook my head. My mind was suddenly empty of all thought.

'Chained, I think,' he said soothingly. 'It makes it easier. Even the most ardent girl can only stand so much.'

He lifted my hands and crossed them at the wrists, then bound them with a gold chain such as had been used on Alice. Perhaps it was the same one; he took it from his pocket. Then he led me toward the centre of the room where, I now saw, there was another hook-and-line arrangement, with a cleat by the door. They lifted my arms as they had Alice's but he stopped them before I had to go on tiptoe; I actually felt quite comfortable there! But numb. My heart had ceased to race and my stomach had nowhere left to fall.

He left me like that and busied himself with the other

146

arrangements. He put out all the lights in the half of the room I was facing. And then I noticed that there was a large mirror on the wall in front of me and I could see everything that was going on behind. They were taking off their coats and rolling up the sleeves of their shirts and pushing the big leather chairs out of the way – making a space where they could take a good run at me. And I could see it all – those dark shapes of devils against the flames! Every time one of them would come in at me, or just stood there and thrashed away, I'd be able to see it coming.

The Marquis returned to me then and stood as he had promised, just in front of me. He was naked from the waist down and I could feel his tool pressing against my mound. He cupped his hands round my breasts and began to caress them. At the same time he murmured in my ear: 'They will not hit you above the small of your back nor below the knee. Of course, if you wriggle and squirm, you will add to their pleasure but it will make their aim difficult. If you can discipline yourself to hold still – and I'll be here to help – that is the only place you'll be hurt.'

'Will they . . .' I could not ask it.

But again he knew. 'Not one of them will break your skin. To shed blood is, among us, a matter of the poorest taste. Now open up and let me get inside you, there's a sweet child.'

I could not believe it. That primal union of man and woman, which had become the very core of my life and being during this past year . . . here! In circumstances such as this! But it happened. I dumbly opened my thighs and let him in!

One of the masters came forward and gently laid his implement against the back of my thighs. 'This is the leather-covered stock, mademoiselle,' he said. 'He makes

147

a heavy, dull sort of impact and the pain from him is diffuse. I shall try to be gentle to start with.'

He took me completely by surprise. I had expected him to back away and take a run – especially after all those preparations. But quick as a flash he raised it where he stood and brought it down hard against the very top of my buttocks.

'Hah!' I gave out one shriek of pain and astonishment.

'Remember, these are Acts of Love,' the Marquis went on whispering, moving himself slowly in and out of me all the time.

Another came forward. 'Here's young Hazel,' he laughed. 'She gives a bright, merry sting that soon passes and leaves you with quite a glow.'

I tensed, ready for it, but he walked off and gave himself the pleasure of a long run at me, taking advantage of the lightness of his switch to deliver me a mighty sting.

Again I cried out.

After that there was a long pause. The Masters went on talking among themselves and the Marquis went on quietly working away. I felt nothing. That alone told me all I needed to know about myself and these games. I would never be one of them. And my refusal would not be out of moral choice, not because 'I would rather die than do that', but because there was nothing there within me to respond – no golden seed. Now it was just a matter of surviving this ordeal and talking the Marquis into letting me go back to my beloved Comte.

One by one they came up and introduced their instruments to me – the cane, the riding crop, the dressage whip, the birch. Each caressed my skin with it before he took his whack. There were such long pauses between each one that I lost count of the number of strokes I took. I know there came a point where I stopped screaming –

when they all came at me in one swift flurry, bang, bang, bang . . . And, of course, I could not prevent myself from squirming around, trying to avoid their torture. That made it impossible for the Marquis to stay inside me, so he wandered away, sat down in a chair, and watched. But one of the others was so roused at the sight of my wriggling little *derrière* he rushed forward and took me from behind while the others laughed and cheered him on. Several others followed suit. I don't know whether Miss Laycock or Miss Brown played hostess but I had no feeling anywhere there by now.

At last it was over. They left me hanging there quite a while before they let me down; during that time they lit their cigars and poured out the port and brandy and told each other obscene jokes. The Marquis, fully dressed again, strode to the door and flung it open. The swiftness of his act revealed all the Slaves pressed against it, straining to catch the thwack of my flesh and the screams I made. They backed away and milled around in embarrassed terror.

'You may take her to her cell,' he told Alice and Charlotte.

The others remained behind, excited beyond measure by my pain.

Alice stayed with me all night, cradling me in her arms. In fact, I did not go out of that cell for the best part of a week. She left me only when one of the Masters sent word that he wanted her; otherwise she was constantly at my side. I think it was plain to them all by now that I was a Mistake, and they did not really know what to do with me next. The Marquis wouldn't send me back home because that would have been like admitting his failure to the Comte, whose philosophy he dismissed as 'pretty little girls and boys playing in the sun'. But he didn't know what to do with me, either.

149

Alice didn't talk about it until that week was up; then it was I who broke our silence. I mean we had been silent on that particular topic but we had chattered away like magpies on everything else under the sun. I am never low-spirited for long – nor angry, nor vindictive, nor jealous, nor anything like that. I don't have the depth of character for it I suppose. I was very sore for two days; then just sore; then tender; and so, by the end of the week – though my skin looked absolutely *dreadful*, all blue and brown and purple, there was nothing under it but discomfort. In fact, you know that final stage of healing, where scratching a sore is rather pleasant? Well, it was just like that.

Then I felt able to say to Alice, 'Tell me the difference between you and me.'

She made a hopeless sort of gesture, as if it were something she had tried to explain to herself a hundred times without success. 'It's the way I am. It took me a long time to recognize it – and even longer to admit it. If I hadn't met the Marquis . . .' Again that shrug.

'And are you happy?'

'Oh, it's much deeper than happiness.'

'Then I shall never understand it.'

She nodded sadly at the truth of that.

'When you made that extra confession,' I reminded her, 'about lascivious feelings toward me – do you have them still?'

'Yes.'

We took off our clothes and lay for a while, me, the lighter, on top of her. And then we did all those things we girls at the Château C. used to do when there was no man immediately available to us. What I thought was so marvellous about Alice was that, being forbidden to wear perfume, she was *all* Woman. She had fragrances I had forgotten, and my climax, when it came (remember, I had

150

gone a whole week without – which had not happened with me since the age of nine!) almost shook me in pieces. Then we curled up in each other's arms again and fell asleep, like babes.

'There,' I said when we were awake once more. 'There was no pain in that.'

'But I knew there would be if one of *Them* had caught us,' she said artfully.

'And without that knowledge you couldn't possibly have enjoyed it at all?' I asked scornfully.

She would not admit I was right, but she would not deny it, either.

'You should come and join us at the Château C.,' I told her. 'You'd very quickly realize what you're all missing here.'

Soon after that I went back to join their daily round. I resumed their strange, Puritan habit – and all their other strange habits, too. I was obedient and submissive and all they could wish for – not out of fear, for something told me they wouldn't whip me again unless I gave them the most flagrant cause; I just made an unspoken pact with them that I'd give no further trouble and at the end of my month I'd say, 'Well, I almost like it, but not quite enough', and put it all down to experience and leave it at that.

'Playing their game' involved this absurd rule about being available to any of the Masters at any time, day or night, and so forth. What it boiled down to in practice was a quick, joyless coupling in a corridor or out in the shrubbery, where you weren't allowed to show your pleasure or be loving or anything like that. You, the woman, were just a *thing*, a mere object of Man's lust, which is something I have never felt in all my years as a Lady of Pleasure.

Poor Masters! I was so sorry for them – all the beautiful

Joys they were missing. And the really infuriating part was that you couldn't *tell* them. It's the sort of thing you have to show rather than tell.

However, there was this one young fellow (I refuse to call him Master now) who really lit a fire in me; I shivered with lust just to look at him. And I knew from watching her that Fleur was in the same lamentable way. So one day, when he came to me and barked the usual things: 'Up behind!' and 'Bend over', and all that, I let him poke me two or three times and then, standing up and spinning round, took his tool in my skilful and ardent fingers while I whispered in my most seductive voice, 'If you'll come upstairs to Fleur's room in half an hour . . .'

'Who's Fleur?' he pretended.

'. . . and forget all this stupid Master-Slave nonsense, we'll show you, Fleur and I – we'll show you voluptuous delights you've never dreamed were possible.'

He gulped. His eyes went wide with alarm. I could see the last shreds of his will fighting his overwhelming lust . . . or no, not lust. Out of respect for the Marquis, let's call it his libido. Anyway, he had no chance.

But I was taking a chance, for I hadn't discussed the idea with Fleur at all. In the end, I didn't risk telling her; I just pretended I had come to her room for the usual little bit of amatory dalliance with her – of which we'd had a few by then. She was willing enough, as always. 'Drop-of-a-hat' would have been a better nickname for her. (And 'Hat' was a good pet name for her quim, too, for it was often *felt*!)

We'd both had a couple of climaxes by the time he arrived. Being a Master, he just burst in without knocking. Being a Man, he just stood there and gawped.

Fleur was on the point of falling back into her Slave role when I whispered in her ear, 'Let's give him a

Loving he'll never forget!' I was spooned behind her at the time, with my fingers on her nipples and bud, so she didn't linger over her agreement.

Well! When the Marquis caught us four hours later, he was absolutely livid! I never saw a man so beside himself with fury. And poor little . . . I've forgotten his name. Let's call him Armand. God, I think that *was* his name! How does it lie there like that, dormant in my mind all those years . . . after all those other men? Anyway, poor little Armand, was quite sure he'd be wearing a golden chain between us about his wrists that night.

'I'll give you the cat for this,' the Marquis spat at me.

It was the worst of all their Punishments, the only one where they broke their rule and drew blood. And when it was over, every one of them ravished the Slave in the vilest way they could think of.

'I'll go down to my cell,' I said as if in submission. I didn't wish to argue with him then and there, but I knew he'd follow me down when he was cooler; I knew he wouldn't go from this to a Punishment like that without trying to gloat. And now I knew I was ready for him.

Sure enough, an hour later, he was there. I was lying on my bed (those 'cells' were not very spartan), naked, face down. He drew up a chair and sat beside me, reaching out his hand to stroke me all down my spine. 'This beautiful flesh,' he murmured. 'Tonight it will be in shreds and tatters.'

'No it won't,' I murmured back. 'If you've got a shred or a tatter of sense left, this beautiful flesh will be in a carriage and on its way back to the Château C.'

He went on stroking me and I heard him easing himself out of his clothes with his other hand. I let a little silence grow and then I added, 'And even then – even if

153

you're wise enough to let me go tonight – you know who'll already be coming with me?'

He laughed at the very idea.

'Armand, for one,' I went on relentlessly. 'Alice for two.' The hand stopped its stroking. 'Fleur for three.' The hand grabbed up a fistful of my flesh. I braced myself for the pain and concluded, 'And Gudrun for four! But give me another two weeks and I'll take the lot.' (I forgot to mention that I had enjoyed quite a few Bouts of Pleasure with pretty young Gudrun, too.)

It cost me all my self control to prevent myself from screaming out.

I don't think he even noticed my stoicism; he was just gripping me the way anyone might grip a railing, or a blanket, in a moment of intense emotion. Then he laughed. 'Oh, mademoiselle, you have no idea of the forces you are trying to tamper with. Armand would be no loss. You're welcome to him. But as to those women – you know nothing of the deep and powerful forces that bind them to me – to this house.'

'But there you are wrong, M. le Marquis,' I said. 'It is not your fault, but when it comes to matters carnal, you are, after all, only a man – and men have so little to think with in that department. You think with the tip of your tool. But a woman can think all over. D'you want to make it a challenge? Forget this silly flogging tonight. Just give me my other two weeks – and then you'll see how many of your Slaves will stay. I dare you.'

'What nonsense!' he exclaimed, but he did not return to the attack.

It wasn't nonsense, though. Women *are* almost infinitely malleable in carnal matters. And that – though he was too stupid to see it – was how he succeeded with his Slaves. Fleur was the most blatant example. If you poured a barrel of cold, slimy frogs and toads all over her while she was enjoying a really fine climax – and did it often enough – she'd soon be swearing that cold, slimy frogs and toads were the most erotic things in the universe. That's how he'd bent them all to his will – or someone else had, back in their childhood or when they were young girls. Someone had taught them to think of Pain and Love as twins. Perhaps even a caning from a loving father could do it. I don't know. Nobody ever caned me until my first night in that dreadful place.

Of course, I had prepared all these arguments while I was waiting for him down there in my cell. What I had not been prepared for was the possibility that he might try that very trick out on me. While I was lying there, putting the final polish, so to speak, on my thoughts and wondering how to steer the conversation round to them, he had taken off his clothes. Now he climbed on top of me, from behind. He was hot and stiff as a ram already and put it in without ceremony. It took my breath away.

Perhaps I ought not to tell you this but, of all the truly exquisite pleasures available to a Woman – and I don't mean those jolly, prankish romps, or true and deep affairs of the heart – I mean those *exquisite* pleasures in which the highest portions of our mind remain aloof, savouring the experience – of all *those* pleasures the very cream is to be roused and then well and truly rogered by a skilful, devious, lusty man whom you absolutely *hate*! Now I couldn't begin to explain it. I don't think a man could even understand it. But there it is. You can take it as warning or encouragement; that's up to you.

Very soon after he started I was running with sweat, climaxing and climaxing and climaxing – and begging him for mercy. And that was when he started to hurt me – not crudely with bites and knuckles, but subtly, by squeezing certain joints and tendons and all those anatomical things we have inside us.

155

Thank God I'd thought it out beforehand, else I would never have withstood him. That blend of pleasure, the most intense I'd felt in a long time, coupled with the most subtle forms of pain was . . . again, I have to use that word, *exquisite*. If he had done this to me while that flogging had gone on, by heaven, I think I'd have made his best recruiting sergeant instead!

Desperately I tried to think of a way out. Not as a man thinks but as a woman – with my body, as I had told him. And, of course, my body gave me her answer: my Special Squeeze. Now I let him have it as never before. Miss Laycock's throat became an urgent, sucking, gorging, ravenous vacuum. Even if he had been limp, she'd still have sucked the milt out of him. And he, of course, was too intent upon his own cunning tricks to notice it. They *do* think with the tips of their tools; so by the time his milt came knocking at that particular brain, it was much too late.

'No!' he cried in horror, and I felt him trying to pull out.

But muscles more ancient than any he knew of kept him there, kept him ramming, ramming, into that greedy maw of my hole. Had he ever spent into a woman before? By his surprise I think not, I'm sure he had not. The quantity was vast. It gurgled in a sticky, unpleasant way when he at last went limp and fell half out of me. And he was exhausted. More – he was defeated.

More still – he was dead.

He just lay there, with his whole world shattered around him.

And then I did one of the few cruel things I've ever done in all my life – deliberately cruel, I mean (for I'm sure I've broken a lot of quickly mended hearts by my inability to love only one man at a time): I stroked his face gently, as *if* I were truly sorry for what I'd done, and I murmured,

'And now, *mon cher M. le Marquis*, are *you* coming to the Château C. tonight as well?'

Every yours, sweet nymph,
Frances
Comtesse de C.

LETTER TEN

FROM MOUNT VENUS,
Wednesday, 24th April, 1850

Sweet Fanny,
 Well then, where was the ghost of me? Nowhere. I've been barking up a chimera all these years. Nevertheless, the search for her has been so exhausting these past days that, now I'm back into my regular Sunday-Wednesday writing habits, I don't really want to start my tale again, not so soon. I'm exhausted, that's what.
 So I think I'll respond to an earlier request of yours and tell you all those words you asked for. I'm going to disgust myself, having to write them down, but, short of sending you to live in a House of Pleasure for a year – and hiding you under the beds, to boot – I do see your

point. There's no other way you can acquire them. So (swallowing my distaste) here I go.

Let's begin with all the words I can think of for that wonderful, tyrannical, soft-hard, urgent, overpowering object of our destiny – a man's tool. Without it, not only are we all at a loss, in every way, but I think life would not be worth living. If angels don't have them, I don't want to go to heaven. Here are the things he gets called: Abraham; old Hornington; *arbor vitae*; baby-maker; belly ruffian; bit of snug; bone; bowsprit; boyo; cock; cracksman; creamstick; culty gub; dick; Dr Johnson (who, as you know, would *stand up* to anyone!); handstaff; dreadnought; flapper; eye-opener; generating tool; gravy giver; girlometer; gristle; horn; holy poker; jigger; jiggle bone; John Thomas; knob; ladies' lollipop; lullaby; machine; old man; the Member for Hairyfordshire; merry maker; Nebuchadnezzar (because he eats 'grass', another name for our bush); Nimrod; old Adam; pecker; pego; pestle; piledriver; plug tail; Polyphemus; pride of the morning; ramrod; rantallion; rhubarb; rogerer; root; rumpsplitter; stargazer; sternpost; sugar stick; sweetmeat; tackle; tallywag; tantrum; tickletail; tool; weapon.

Of course, there are other names – whore's names, which I will not use, such as pr*ck, c*ck, d*ck, and so on. If you follow my plan you shall live a long life, as full of Pleasure as mine, and never hear them.

Our upper charms are called apple dumplings; the baby's pub; blubber; hemispheres; cabman's rest; cream jugs; dairies; dugs; globes; heavers; Cupid's kettledrums; milky way; top buttocks; upper works – and the nipples are cherrylets. But I think there is no word so dainty and exciting as breasts.

The seat of *our* delight, Miss Laycock, has the following soubriquets: Abraham's bosom; the monosyllable; centre of bliss; chink; agreeable ruts of life; civet; cleft; hairy

160

oracle; Hairyfordshire; hole; Miss Horner; holloway; holey of holeys; home sweet home; honeypot; hortus; blind alley; Hornington Crescent; lapland; love lane; low country; mill; bottomless pit; moey; pussy; muff; notch; novelty; old hat; open sea (c for c*nt); commodity; parsley bed; periwinkle; placket; pleasure boat; purse; crack; portable property; quim; quoniam; red ace; rose; sampler; scut; crevice; seed bed; seminary; slit; standing room for a man; sucker; crown and feathers; sportsman's gap; tail gate; teazle; thatched house; cuckoo's nest; temple of Hymen and low men; tipperary fortune; titbit; cunny; touch hole; tu quoque; whim; cut-and-come-again; dumb glutton; upright grin; fumblers' feast; Cupid's furrow; the gape above the garter; gash; old mossyface.

Her adornment is: moss; fleece; feathers; dilberry bush; fluff; furbelow; furze; grass; grove; plush; quim bush (or whiskers or wig); scut; shaving brush; shrubbery; silent beard; tail feathers. A false one is a merkin.

Again, there are such whore's words as c*nt, gr*wl, pr*tt, g*v*l, h*t b**f, m*ntr*p, tw*t, and the like. The worst of all is that our own name – f*nny – is also perverted to name her, which I do not think in the least bit funny. Again, the life of a Lady of Pleasure is possible without such knowledge.

Our amorous tricks and dallying is termed thus: feel the way to heaven; huffle; play hot cockles; come aloft; dildo; fiddle; fork her; in full fig; full on for it; get above her garter; hornify; itch; lick-spigot or larking; skin the live rabbit (being pulling back a man's foreskin, which is an intense pleasure to him if done daintily); turn up her tail; tip the velvet; wander in the milky way . . . oh, there are too many here; you will not mistake them when you hear them said.

*　　*　　*

161

The Lovely Act itself, that pinnacle of supremest joys is called: addition; put 4 quarters on the spit; horizontal refreshment; cure the horn; take on beef; bit of snug; block or caulk her; see stars while lying on her back; cram her; diddle her; dip his wick; dive in the dark; knee trembler; perpendicular; dog her; fettle her; fit end to end; fore and aft her; four-legged frolic; make free at both ends; frig; get among her frills; get outside of him; join giblets; give her a shot; take a turn in Hair Court; feed the dumb glutton; grind; work the hairy oracle; have a bit of hard; give hard for soft; give him a hole to hide in; have a hot roll with cream; hump; play in and in; jigajig; jump; lift a leg over her; make ends meet; melting moments; double his milt; all there but most of him; nooky; occupy her; get outside him; peg her up; matrimonial polka; pray with her knees up; quiff; rake her out; brush her flue or work for chimney-sweeps; rantum scrantum; rod; roger; scour; shoot her in the tail; shake a coat of skin; slip her a length; a squeeze and a squirt; take the starch out of him; strum; stuff her; give the old man his meat or supper; swive; measure the inside of her; pocket the red; hole in one.

The whore's word is f*ck or sh*g, which I have never spoken and never shall. Also scr*w, which I have used in contempt for a kind of loving I despise.

The crowning and climax of that Loving Act is: shoot between wind and water; come off; cream; ease himself; fetch; fire a shot; fall in the furrow; goose grease her; gravy; honey; jelly; jet his juice; light her lamp; give her juice for jelly; make her chimney glow; melt; melted butter; mettle; milk; milt; oil of horn; ointment; roe; shoot the bishop; shoot white; shoot over the stubble (when he pulls out and wets your navel instead); wet her bottom; give her a bottom-wetting; tail juice; make a settlement in tail . . . again, too many to mention. You will know it when it happens to you and you will make your own dulcet words for it then.

But why, dear heart, do you wish to know the words that whores are called? I give them you because I can deny you nothing (except a further chance for your mother to ruin me), but please put them from your mind at once.

A whore is a: bangtail; Bankside lady; bat; bed presser; bit of muslin; buttock; cat; cocktail; Columbine; Covent Gdn lady; cyprian; doe; Drury Lane vestal; fem; flash tail; gay bit; girl of ease; guinea hen; horizontale; ladybird; bobbity; lone dove; open tail; merrylegs; moll; mort; quail; receiver general; squirrel; wagtail; public ledger (because entered daily) . . .

And here are a few that slip through your neat categories:

Horn pills are aphrodisiacs; a randy man is born with a horn; an old lecher is (by a transfer of initial sounds) a buck fitch – you might also call him cunny haunted; those lozenges I use to augment my natural juices and stop the babies are, by some, called dreadnaughts; milt is also called discharged seamen (because it fills our navel basins!); jealous friends have sometimes called me 'loose in the hilt or rump' – I would deny it utterly . . . indeed, I think I did in one of these letters; a toast in the old days was, 'Here's to the inside of woman and the outside of gaol'; another – 'Here's to both ends of the busk!' (or, nowadays, 'corset'); a girl who says she will and then reneges is a c*ck-teaser; to be caught *in flagrante* is to be caught with rem in re; a lady who raises her skirts to warm her *derrière* at the hearth is 'heating up her old man's supper'; a man who cannot keep out of women is a beard splitter . . . has Irish toothache . . . is a knocker . . . a lapful . . . a meatmonger . . . a pullet squeezer . . . a table-end man . . . c*ntstruck . . . so many words for them, whom I call simply 'darling'. But no word for me, who is as amorous and 'tool-struck' as any among 'em!

Now complain my letters have grown too long!

Ever yours, sweet nymph,
Frances
Comtesse de C.

LETTER ELEVEN

FROM MOUNT VENUS,
Sunday, 26th May, 1850

Sweet Fanny,

Yes, 'tis more good sense to wait for your letters, in between mine, than to go hastening on and to get so far ahead of you. But had I not made such a rush at my memories of the Maison Q., I doubt I should have topped the hurdle at all. Still, that is now behind me – or will be when I have told you what became of those liberated Slaves, which I shall anon.

First, however, I must interject that I am astonished at your latest requests. The *most* number of men that ever rogered me in the space of one twenty-four hours? The *most* number of climaxes I ever experienced in the same time? The *most* I ever procured in my Lovers? The *longest* single Act of Love I ever enjoyed? The *biggest* tool I ever accommodated in each of my Holes? The *greatest number* of Lovers I ever let at me in the one Passage of Arms? . . . Your list goes on and on.

Dear Fanny, what is this sudden fascination with superlatives? Who or what has put such notions into your mind – surely nothing I have writ? Oh, my Sweet Child, have you not understood me yet? The Delight that fills the life of a Lady of Pleasure to overflowing does not reside in these Battle Honours. How should it seem if above my Couch of Voluptuous Bliss I should hang a banner with (for example):

Tower of Happy Maidens, 7 July 1817
Old White's Club, 14 Feby 1819
Mrs Featherstonehaugh's Academy, 4 Janry 1824
Ld N-ll's Coach on road to A-ck, 29 November 1827
Office of M. le Président de la 2me République, 1 Mai 1832 . . .

. . . and so forth, as our regiments of soldiers do on their banners? If ever you tried such a thing, I promise you, you'd mourn the time lost – time that could all be your Glee and Gratification, but that you must instead waste in explaining to your Lover what and when and how. And, Men being what they are (bless 'em), he would only seek to outdo the rest and prick his colour on your chart. So I do beseech you, put all such ideas from your mind. I, for my part, shall not deign to answer you.

And let me kill the notion once and for all by answering the first on your list – since, as you point out, I have already done so in an earlier letter (I had forgot that). Yes, it is true that, at Old White's Club on Sunday the 14th day of February, 1819 (I being then 19, too, of course, and some four years experienced in all the Arts and Wiles of Voluptuousness), I was rogered in one evening by the entire membership of that club, which incident arose out of a chance remark I let drop the week before. It is also true that many a Covent Garden blowsabella could boast of more – indeed one vaunted to me of having 'done' sixty in one evening, in a bush in Hyde Park in the Summer after Waterloo; but when I asked her if she, too, had *taken* her pleasure of each and every one (which was part of *my* bargain with *my* thirty-five), why, her jaw dropped to her navel and she stared at me in abject askancement. (And her friend later told me in confidence that 'twas not sixty, anyway, but only fifty-eight – so they are liars and cheats, those whores, who have not the first notion of giving or receiving value. All they do is trade milt for gold. Fie, I say!) (Actually, with them, 'tis not gold but copper – and robbery at that.)

But why have you got me onto this? Oh yes – 'twas to tell you that such a prankish romp as that was nothing but folly, the giddy inspiration of a lusty young girl, hungry for every kind of erotic sensation, and thinking she might find it in such superlatives – those same superlatives as lately seem to obsess you, my dearest grandchild. I was perturbed beyond measure when I read your list of queries, for I could see you – in your *imagination*, as yet, I trust – taking the same barren path as I, all those years ago. So I abjure you – turn aside now. Voluptuous fulfilment is to be found elsewhere. In your case, I hope it will be found – now this will perturb you, but read on – you will laugh at the end, I promise. In your case, I hope and pray you will discover that all the bounteous Pleasures that Eros can bestow in such overflowing abundance on us fortunate Females will be found not a dozen miles from here: in the Maison Q!

What? That vile place? Grandmama dear, what do you take me for?

Read on, dear heart.

Of those Slaves: Hortense and Annette discovered they lov'd each other more than any Man; they took a small house not a league from here and have lately (1848) completed the tenth edition of their Flora of this province; they dine with us from time to time. Such fine, dear women they are, too. Charlotte stayed on at the Château Q. and completed her restoration of the tapestries; she has since woven two more, each taking over a decade to make; we meet often enough, too – though not socially; curiously, she, also, has lately published a Manual on her *oeuvre*, which is said to be the finest ever. Alice, Gudrun, and lazy, sensual little Fleur all came back with me to the Château C. – where my dear Comte received them with *Showers* of Love and Joy! Fleur is now, I hope, serving ambrosia and tickling the tool or *cutte* of every Angel in Heaven, but Alice and Gudrun live here still, in cottages in our grounds; both are blissfully married. (I never knew anyone, man or woman, who devoted themselves ardently to sensual pleasure, who lived mean and died miserable; we are the Children of the Gods. 'Children who live in the Sun', as poor old Q. used to sneer.)

Millie came with us, too, but not to take up our 'life in the Sun'. Her True Passion in life was horses – though, as she rode split-on-the-saddle as often as she could, I tell you I had my own Suspicions there! But, to each his own. 'Tis a great big world, and who has authority to say *only* this or *only* that? She has made our stables the Mecca of all Europe, among those whose Passions are also equine in leaning. Ah me, time was when the name 'Château C.' meant 'fillies' of a very different colour – and a more thrilling kind of 'riding', too!

And the Marquis de Q? Well, all the world now knows what became of him.

He blamed the Comte. He said I was a bomb with a

two-week fuze deliberately sent to wreck his House. Did you ever hear anything more absurd? How could he forget he had me chained and helpless, and stood there rogering me while six of his cronies flogged me half to death? And he dared call *me* a threat to *him*! No, the truth was – and did he not tell me so in his very own words? – that House was steeped in Illusion and Paradox. 'Twas a house of playing cards such as children build on the nursery floor on rainy days. One glimpse of the Sunshine and 'tis forgot; then any little puppy or stray draught of wind may knock it down without complaint. Bomb, indeed! I was much more like a puppy, wagging my little tail, and with my tongue ever out, panting for new fun every day. Men do so love to dramatize single events into great, earthshaking cataclysms; but, poor things, we who have so many shots in our locker should not grudge them the illusion, I suppose.

Anyway, 'twas not by day or by Sunshine we returned, but by darkest, warmest night – Gudrun, Fleur, Alice, and I. We had all taken the sweetest Pleasure of each other by then, many times, but all the way over I told them our Joys were as tedious as sermons (you will need to have heard French Protestant sermons to feel the full force of this simile) compared with the Delights that lay in store for them beneath my darling C. – and on him, and before him, and beside him, and *soixante-neuf* with him ... They were panting like gazelles when we arrived.

So, too, of course, was I! And I had ten thousand times more reason, for I *knew* whereof I spoke. And Miss Laycock knew. And my breasts and nipples knew. And my ardent little *derrière* ... my hips, the backs of my knees ... my every little tuck and frill ... we all knew. And we were determined to race ahead by a secret way I had learned, and so get at that darling man before them.

169

But in my blind, feverish haste, I took the wrong way and came out in a part of the Château I had never seen before – or not (as I at once discovered) from inside. What aided that discovery was the sight of a pensive young man, sitting in a window enclosure, reading a book. (Aristotle's *Poetics*, in case I have inflam'd your fancy into suspicions of something more incandescent.) He was, of course, young François, the Comte's son, whom I had seen staring so wistfully at the Tower of Happy Maidens over a year ago.

I was then turned seventeen, not quite fully formed but much more so than when I first arrived. He was of the same age, too, almost to the day, as I have said; and believe me, he had *everything* a young man ought and all as perfectly formed as a young maid could wish. You think I refer to his physical parts alone? Not so. Splendid as they were, he had one attribute more that outweighed all the rest: virginity! When a man has reached the age of seventeen, never knowing the feel of a woman though being kept daily in the sight and sound of them . . . well! Now there *is* a bomb – and the fuze has been all those *years* a-burning!

So our eyes met and our knees trembled and we raced out of our clothes and rogered and spent within ten seconds flat? Ha ha! I have read those stupid books. No, Sweet Fanny, we did nothing that first evening – burning with lust as I was. I think we hardly touched. But a *pact* was joined. Our eyes invoiced consignments of unimaginable pleasures that our poor, overworked, tormented bodies would take a year to deliver.

Yes, but what actually *happened*, I hear you ask? I never knew such a one for wanting to know times, dates, places, who touched who first, where, what the feeling . . . These things do not signify. The Pleasures of Love ride on a warm, heaving sea of electricity; to hear your

170

Lover clear his throat behind you could easily be the most erotic act of the entire evening. Until you have felt the burning Desire that can turn anything and everything in the world to a miniature *tressaillement*, you have not even begun to understand it.

So what actually happened that first evening was that we fell in Love. And I was as shy and confused and nervous as any virgin who ever lived. It is true! I who had just come from those unspeakable bestialities at the Maison Q., still hot with shame at my climax with its dreadful owner, I blushed and stammered and longed to touch and dared not touch and looked away and spoke of the most boring trivialities when all I really wanted was to throw my arms about his neck and smother his beautiful lips with kisses . . . and surrender.

So what we actually did that evening was to talk of his life and upbringing, his hopes, his ambitions! Oh, what a sweet, solemn little man he was, my darling François. It was the Comte's idea to bring him up in the way he himself had been reared: very strict and utterly, utterly serious. How stupid are those (I can say this because the Comte himself will admit it now, at long last) how stupid they are who wish to force another generation along the tramlines of their own. That is why I merely suggest to you that you might like to try this or try that – and give it up at once if 'tis not to your taste. To learn what you do *not* like is as important a knowledge of yourself as what you do. Was not that the lesson I brought back from the Maison Q? And had it not been the Comte's purpose in sending me there?

But he would not be like that with his own son. He did not say, as I say to you, 'Try this dish of pheasant, if you will. I liked it at your age, so you may do so, too. If not, the rest of the board is there for your selection still'. No. He said, 'Eat this pheasant or be damned!'

171

But in his defence I'll say that 'twas no impulse to tyranny in him that made him so; rather it was a too-cunning cleverness. For he had been brought up strict, out of the company of desirable females, had broken out and fallen into the arms of a voluptuous maid, and between them they devised his beautiful philosophy. (In fact, she became his first Comtesse and was the mother of this very lad. And I can think of no finer tribute to her memory than that the Comte did *not* mope and shut himself away at her death but decided to spread his philosophy as wide as . . . what shall I say? As wide as the thighs of the hundreds of girls who later drank in their learning at that Inexhaustible Fount!)

Anyway, 'twas my Comte's notion that if the youth had any C. spunk in him, he, too, would break out in the same manner and find some equally Ardent Maid . . . and so give the whole cycle one more spin. He believes that Shakespeare made poor work of Romeo and Juliet, for he thinks the Montagues and Capulets of the parental generation actually conspired together to make the ardent couple *believe* there was a feud between them – and only later fell out in earnest. Which, if you think on't, would be a far more stirring Tragedy than the preordained thing Shakespeare served, where, from curtain-up you may easily guess the stage hands will have blood to mop up by the bucket ere they sup their beer that night. For once, that is no digression of mine, for it is the very Tragedy that was soon to overwhelm me and bring to an end my days in the Tower of Happy Maidens.

As I listened to my darling François, telling me of his dreams – and begging me with the mute pleadings of his eyes to peer beyond them and fathom quite different desires, which he could not name – I realized I understood more of his father's purpose than did he; for he knew only its effect, which was to cramp and confine him there; I, however, knew its purpose as well – which was to goad him to rebellion. Now I thought (and indeed think so still) that was as good as a command to me to assist the young man, don't you? The Comte still will not admit it – though he smirks in his denial. (You can never push a man *all* the way home when the name of that home is Truth, *nota bene*!)

So that first evening all we achieved in the way of Amatory advance was a promise to meet the following night at that same hour and place. Oh, and he kissed my hand!

The Comte, with hindsight, says he should have noticed the easy way I yielded him to the Charms of our three new fillies from the Maison Q. At the time he thought me still shaken from my ordeal. Of course, we enjoyed a mighty rogering together that night; but at any other time it would have been a dozen, nor would he have slept. But there it was, my one, restrained (for me) outing in that old, familiar Paradise did no more than prick on my Desires for my sweet young virgin boy.

You remember how gentle the Comte was at my induction and initiation into the ravishing transports of the voluptuary world? Well, 'twas exactly so, with roles reversed, between young François and me. There is a small pavilion here, down by the lake. Remember – we made little paper boats there once, you and I, and watched the stormy zephyrs dash them to shreds on the merciless reeds? Well, I remember it, anyway. And I remember, too, as I watched your dear little head, with its darling tresses, bent so solemnly over your hands as they tried to make the folds . . . I remembered the hours and hours of indescribable pleasure young François and I enjoyed in that same spot; and I wondered where and when it would be your turn to cross that same divide and taste the nectars of Eros in that Paradise he has built for

173

us on Earth. Dare I hope now it will be in that same delightful pavilion? And soon?

Certes, few places in this world are better fashioned for it, especially if the season be summer and the nights all balmy and warm. We wandered thither in a kind of dream, hand in hand, saying nothing, yet knowing full well what we were about to do. The marble table there, as you remember, is enormous; and the cupboards are filled with silken cushions and quilts of finest down. The moon was almost full and, by the time we arrived there, our eyes were so accustomed to the dark we could see each other as well as it were day. He sat and watched me arrange it all; nor did I hurry, knowing well how his anxieties (with which he was shot through and through) needed scope in which to die. And I knew, too, how a Man loves to watch a Woman move about him, especially if he knows he will soon be inside her. When we lean forward to place a cushion just so, all they can see is our breasts hanging down; we bend over to smooth a quilt, never for one moment realizing we thereby make an artless offering of our delicious little *derrière*; we lift the hem of our dress to remove a small splinter from our ankle . . . and the intimations of *heaven's above*! drive them wild with lust. We move near them, stirring the air, and we leave behind a fragrance of ourselves powerful enough to forge the shackles of a lifelong slavery.

I have often envied the Men this easy faculty for arousal; they can exercise it with almost anything in skirts. (Else neither the Lady of Pleasure nor her counterfeit the whore would find scope!) True, we can find it as easily with some of them, but for the most part we must go about it more slowly.

Be that as it may, poor young François, by the time I had disposed our bed to my satisfaction, was shivering at the heat of that summer's night and choking on a surfeit of its balmy air. Remember, we had not even kissed as yet – and here was I, preparing to let him hear the music of Pan! It was a scene for any man to dream on.

A standing woman of the same sort of height as a man, a beautiful woman, all perfume and promise, can be a frightening thing to him, especially when her eyes dance in his, and sparkle with the challenge to drown her in Pleasure – and this is so even in a House of Pleasure, when he has come there for that very purpose, and made his choice among its *demoiselles*, and taken her hot and passionate to her chamber. I have seen them die even then. How much greater is that fear when the youth is virgin and the compact between them unconfined!

So you will understand why I lay down upon my quilt and, with a sigh of mild unease, nothing stronger, closed my eyes and loosened the first button of my blouse; to explore *me* as well as my Charms would have been too much. I let him begin in silence, undoing this button, then that, running his trembling fingers over my skin beneath. All I did was sigh, and move a little toward him, as if I could not help myself – which was, indeed, often the case. Oh how I longed to throw all this caution aside and swamp him in my skill; but I remembered how the dear Comte, who, when it came to skill, still had so many greater claims than I, I remembered how he nonetheless held himself back and allowed me to join him at my own pace . . . and so I reined myself in.

When at last he found my nipple, I dared open my eyes and stare up at him in a kind of hooded, dreamy gratitude. Soon he had me so molten it was all I could do to hold my pace back to his. When I lay naked to my waist he began to undo his shirt, too. 'No,' I pleaded softly. 'Don't leave me halfway peeled.'

He blushed to the roots of his scalp and started to fiddle with the fastenings of my skirt. Then I began to talk, to the air about us as much as to him. 'You've no idea how delicious it is to a woman, to be utterly, utterly nude. Are you looking at me, my darling François? Do you like what you see? Is it what you expected? Tell me how it makes you feel . . .' and so on. It was nothing of any moment, just light, playful chatter to set him further at his ease: Virgin Eve to Virgin Adam before their days of Shame. In between I slipped in small words of advice and encouragement – where to caress me, and how, and what variations to try. Oh dear, I feel I'm making this sound so schoolmarmish and it was not at all like that. I was in such a tumultuous fever of longing for him that, by the time he had me fully unclothed, it was all I could do not to throw wide my legs and beg him to leap in, clothed and shod as he was.

Thank heaven he started to undress himself, for it gave me the chance to leap up and tell him he was not to deprive me of that pleasure. But I did not stand a little aloof from him, as he had from me. I laid him on our bed and knelt at his side, or straddled him, or half lay down as I took off his shirt and cravat, his stockings and shoes – everything, in short, but the one garment he was most longing to be rid of. But I prolonged it all I could, not only to satisfy my own enormous lust for his beautiful body, but also to teach him that a Woman does not like to be rushed, even one as ardent as I.

I covered his chest with kisses and tickled his armpits with my busy little tongue and turned him over and massaged his strong, lean back – and let him do the same things to me – all before I even opened his fly. In that way he passed through the high point of his fever for me and settled into a kind of stunned delirium in which time ceased to have its separate moments and everything flowed out of and into everything else. Then I rolled him gently on his back and went at that final barrier.

How tempting it was to straddle him over his chest, *soixante-neuf*, letting Miss Laycock smile down on him, on his gazing, on his exploration! But I knew that the sight of her, blatant and open, can be as alarming to a man as it is enticing. So I kept my knees together, tight against his ribs, on his right, and leaned at a slight diagonal across him – showing him no more than the outer fringe of her two velvety lips. I had arranged matters so that they were all in moonshadow, dark and mysterious. That was mainly because my bruises had not yet quite healed; there was no pain there, just a slight irritation, which, in fact, the touch of another's hand could turn to pleasure.

But even in that dark he noticed it. 'You've had a fall,' he said. 'Do you ride often?'

'As often as ever I can,' I assured him. 'Will you not stroke it better for me?'

And that brought us both to the boil, as he ran his trembling hands oh so gently over those dear folds and crevices, and I eased off his pantaloons.

And that was where I got the most delightful surprise. Until then I think Armand was the youngest Lover I ever enjoyed, and he was fully twenty-three and as well furnished as any I ever met. Between him it was a downward leap of a decade or more to the gardener's boy I had fondled in the vicarage shrubbery at home. He had his first spending with me – one dear little pearly blob that popped out full of pride and surprise and sat in Polyphemus's eye and just begged to be taken up on my tongue. And though I was only twelve, his sweet little pego was quite enclosed in the span of my little-girlish hand. So I had expected, insofar as I had thought of the matter at all – which I hadn't – that François would make me a gift of something in between. Imagine then my delight to find myself staring down at something as well developed and as ruffianly engorged as his father's!

And so hot! 'Twas like a furnace blast around my cheeks. And so throbbing – for those magnificent engines, when they are in that spoiling mood, are an infallible metronome to the beating of their hearts, you know. I sensed from the inflamed look of it he would not be long in spending. I did not dare touch it or brim it over in any way. So with a flash of my tail I was round, and open, and wet – and then hot and snug over him.

And I was just in time, too. For the minute he felt that unique warmth and pressure around him (something that mean-spirited men have tried to forge since the dawn of time – and failed miserably at it, too) he was throbbing and spending as if his milt had Old Father Thames for its well. I was not even flat upon him, but sitting up, the only contact between us being, virtually, the one where all the opposites in the whole erotic world meet and make an Universal Harmony between them. You may think me fanciful for seeking to distinguish between one climax and another, but I tell you, they are as unique to me as every fine dish I ever tasted – and for every one of the latter I had a dozen of the former. So I assure you, I never enjoyed a climax, before or since, that was quite the same as that; but don't ask me to describe it. It was like the taste of new wine, before it has its *embouchure*, or the scent of fresh-cut hay when summer's torpor makes us languorous and even sleeping dogs must put their little crimson carrots out to air, or . . . but no – as I say – I could not possibly describe it.

I looked down and saw tears running off his cheeks. I had seen such a thing in men before – a kind of spontaneous gratitude for delights they had never believed possible. (All men, you know, have dreams of women that would be quite beyond our powers to gratify – or theirs to perform if they even tried it. Countless Lovers have told me so – usually before they add that, of all the women they have known – and how they love to boast of sheer numbers! – I have come closest to helping them make it real.) (And then, of course, I say something vague like, 'The more *this* Lover gives me, the less I need seek or accept from another . . .' and they understand I mean more than the Pleasures we have just found, which has made me as rich in purse as in all my memories of Carnal Delight.)

I stretched myself out upon him then and smothered his face in kisses and asked him why he was miserable. 'Because that is that,' he said, 'and I wished to do so much more. For you, darling *Francesse*' – he always called me that, *François et Francesse*, I think he liked the overtones of heavenly twinship – 'I wanted to please you in so many ways.'

'And what makes you believe you cannot?'

'Well . . .' His tone implied it was surely obvious? He seemed to believe that a climax was *the* climax.

I don't think he even realized he was still stiff as a poker inside me, not until I wriggled a little and he felt Love Lane writhing around him. He gave a little gasp. 'Yes,' I murmured. 'Oh yes, my darling François . . . yes . . . yes.'

He had his father's capacity, too – and I don't know which of us was the more delighted to discover it that night. I lost count of (not that I even started counting) the number of times we came together. I remember rising into a drowsy wakefulness and finding him at it in his sleep, inside me, as firm as ever. But I did not show him all that was possible to us. For instance, we only lay face to face for these revels. Just before dawn, when we would have to rise and go, I lay spooned against him and, with little squirms and a bit of assistance from my fingers, got him into me from behind; but by then we really had drained Old Father Thames quite dry and I didn't

Squeeze him into a painful spending. In fact, I didn't Squeeze him at all that night – oh, there was so *much* we left for another time.

And so 'another time' followed 'yet another time' in which we explored the entire world of sensual delights. It was not every night, of course. I think three nights in the one week was the most we ever managed, and that was in three full months, the happiest months of my life until then – for my Centre of Bliss was still receiving all the Adoration she could get from the darling Comte, and only the fact that he was more often than usual away that summer gave me scope with his son.

At last, of course, the inevitable happened. He brought Alice down to the pavilion one night and caught us. I should have guessed from the fact that the stove was lit, but I assumed my dear, thoughtful François had commissioned it, not his father. Well all the gates of hell were loosed and lightning and thunder rang about us and we were spitted to roast over the pit of the inferno by his tongue. I suppose that, having taught me everything, he expected me to take this meekly as another lesson, too. But I could not help pointing out it ran counter to everything else he had ever said. 'Did you not tell me you wished your son to break his own way out of . . .'

'Yes but not with my wife!' he cried.

'I am not your wife.'

'You are in every important way. I love you as my wife.'

'As you love Alice?' I asked.

He could not deny it, not with her sitting there, listening.

'Yes,' he said, both reluctant and vehement.

'And Elaine? And Nana? And Fleur? And Garence? . . .'

'Yes, yes!' he yelled testily to stop me running the whole gamut – which I would have done.

'So!' I flared back. 'How often have you told us that our passions are all mere private whirlpools in one vast common sea . . .'

'But, dear child . . .'

'And that if we confine them in little private puddles they go rank and stagnant . . .'

'Yes, yes!' he cried out again.

'Well have you told François? Or is it only true for *us*? Does he enjoy no part in our superior type of humanity?'

'But, for the love of Heaven, girl – he's my *son*!'

I laughed. 'Oh yes, my darling – he's your son in every way! Come on now – let's undress and set to and you shall see.'

I truly thought he would die of an apoplexy.

'I've taught him all you ever taught me,' I went on, thinking it would reassure him, but he only sank further into his fit.

Well, that was that. There was no more horizontal refreshment that night. Four days later he sent for me and, in the kindest, gentlest way, told me I must go. He did not blame me. He knew when I came among them I should one day outgrow that place, but it had shaken him to learn the route my Voluptuous Daemon had driven me down.

I said it had driven me up, not down. 'He is as sublime a lover as you.'

He stared at me in a kind of pitying horror. 'Did you truly imagine that he and I might have lain down that night and cavorted with you and Alice?'

I said we had often done such things before, us and his comrades – four and five of us together, male and female at hazard.

This only seemed to confirm him in his decision.

Then I told him I was with child.

I could see the suspicion in his eye at once. '*Your*

child,' I assured him – not that he would ever have voiced a doubt. And, of course, he was nobleman enough to accept it without question and to send me away to his old nurse in P–e for my *enceinture* and *accouchement*. Six months later, in the spring of 1818, your dear mother was born.

The Comte himself did not come to see her. He was afraid I would cast my old spell over him, for he missed the fury of my Carnal Nature grievously. Instead, he sent an old friend of his, an Englishman called Charles D–y – who was, as it happened, a member of the Other White's Club, which was how I went to work there that summer.

What an absurd farrago of tangled emotions it all was! And where is it all now? Not a vestige is left. François, my Lover-stepson, now fifty like me, lives with his wife and ten children at the Château Q. which we rented from the poor Marquis when he went on the first of his many travels to Cathay. He keeps one wing for his own use during his rare visits to France. The Maison Q., deep in the forest, is now a true House of Pleasure, jointly owned by the Comte and François, and all those things the dear man once feared so much he had to banish me to avoid them, they are all of them now . . . well, I cannot say nightly occurrences, nor even weekly nor monthly. Let me say, 'we have our moments still – all of us together'. And I may take a night of frolics at the Maison Q. as the Lady of Pleasure I still am and always shall be as long as my Lovers desire me, which, bless 'em, they do, fit and fifty though I am . . .

Why do I write in this vein – as if I were winding up my tale when there is yet so much to tell? Oh yes, I remember! 'Twas to assure you that relations here are as sweet as they ever were or yet might be. And the man I wish to suggest as the one to take you by the hand and lead you in to that Garden of Earthly Delights and teach you what Indescribable Pleasures and Joys are even now hiding in the secret recesses of your Sweet Young Body is none other than that dear, sweet François for whom I did that same service so long ago.

Well, not *so* long ago. I must not paint him as a buck fitch or horny old lecher. He is as fine and vigorous a Man now as was the Comte when I first met him. He has the same loving regard for Woman, the same almost infinite capacity to Stand and Adore – I tell you, he will send you spinning into Paradise and keep you delirious there for weeks. And then, when you know all the Arts and Possibilities, you can Flesh out your Sentimental Education with a year or two on your back in our House of Pleasure, here, where all our Lovers are Gentlefolk and many bear the oldest names in France.

That, then, is my idea for you. But – as I say – 'tis no prescription but rather a receipt you may try and discard if it be not to your liking. What say you? I think July, which is so hot and spicy and languorous here, is the very prime month for an Ardent Young Girl to lose the burden of her maidenhead. Answer me swiftly, Sweet Fanny, for there will be much to arrange.

Ever yours, sweet nymph,
Frances
Comtesse de C.

LETTER TWELVE

FROM MOUNT VENUS,
Sunday, 9th June, 1850

Sweet Fanny,

Still this obsession with the trivial *externals* of Pleasure – numbers, quantities, places, times, names . . . the most bizarre, the most obscene, the most piquant . . . Why must you know these things? If you were a man, I should understand, for it is the sort of thing that fascinates them endlessly. I saw two men once bet how many pairs of boots each could hang from their tools before collapse. And no, before you even ask, I shall not name the result, for, to tell the truth, I would only be inventing it. What would it signify to a Woman, anyway? All we require is that the thing stand like a good infantryman and *drill* as long as Sergeant Laycock may command it 'On Parade!'

You are tiresome, you know! For the things I wish to tell you now – the things I would have told you in any case – are so close to your endless lists of questions that you will make me *seem* to be answering you, when all I am doing is uttering a warning.

After I had whelped your dear mother, and derived as much pleasure from a mewling, puking, vomiting, shitting, howling little bundle of selfish imperatives as any young mother can, I was as maddened by Lust as after my week with the ivory engine and the Comte away. Charles D–y was so overwhelmed by my capacity for gratification when he came to visit that he flew back to the Other White's without eating or sleeping and made such a breathless report of me that they sent out my fare to London and a gratuity beside by their own courier. And by the end of the month I was enjoying all the Lusty Traffic my dear Miss Laycock could wish for.

The Comte, who had made so many copious settlements in *my* tail, now made one even more generous 'in tail general', as the lawyers say – namely on your dear mother. She, of course, has long since broke the entail and wasted it, for she is as generous with her kind of spending as her father is with his. But to me he offered not a single penny. At the time I thought him mean and vindictive beyond words; now I know it to have been the most generous act of his life. He *gave* me to the world – and he knew the world would reward me lavishly, too. Never, never doubt that man, Sweet Fanny. His wisdom and nobility will turn your meanness back upon you.

The Other White's was a club formed of Old Boys from W–m College; its earliest members, long before my time, had been blackballed (no mere figure of speech in their case) from the Hellfire Club, but the Other White's had quietened down a lot since then and 'twas a very pleasurable House of Joy when I first went to it. Later – not long after I left, in fact – the premises were sold to a man who had won a fortune at Ladbroke's and founded a supper club and dancing rooms there; then it was presided over by the Dowager Marchioness of Q–y, Lady Ell–e, and the redoubtable Mrs B–ft, whose invitations were like gold dust; even the Duchess of D–re, the queen of London Society, would not turn one down. I often used to smile when I read of the Eminent Respectability the place had then acquired, and I wondered whether those who so chastely trod its boards ever realized what Pranks and Follies were once let loose there – many, I am now ashamed to say, by me.

Of course, London in those days was a town of Vice and Pleasure all in one – a filthy town, but ranting, roaring and rambunctious. Do not judge me from the namby-pamby viewpoint of this sickening mid-century – which, believe me, is every bit as vicious underneath its polished skin. There was an openness then in all things concerning our bodily functions. I have walked across Green Park and seen half a dozen Gentlefolk, men and women, shitting in the bushes with scant regard for the passing traffic. Yes! Little Mrs G–dy chatting away twenty to the dozen to the elegant Ld F–y, who obliges her in passing with handfuls of grass and dock leaves to wipe her arse! That was an hourly occurrence. Nowadays one would not write such things, not even cloaking them in sh*t and *rse.

But I have to tell it you so you will comprehend in what general climate of behaviour I was induced to do those awful things.

The Other White's was founded on their elegant ideas of a classical lupanar, the very highest class of a House of Pleasure in Ancient Rome. Everything was done in the most sumptuous taste – not exquisite, as we have managed it here with our refurbishments at the Maison Q. but with that good, solid, English, no-nonsense elegance that produced Chippendale and Adam. Indeed, many is the time I have sat on a Chippendale chair – or, to be precise, on the lap of a Lover on a Chippendale chair – and rogered with such Mighty Ecstasy we almost showered the room below in Adam plaster.

The Club had thirty-five members, never more and never fewer. 'The Committee keeps *our* members topped up – and *their* members keep you Girls topped up,' as the Chairman explained during my first interview (which was almost entirely *à la horizontale*). I thought I had strayed into Paradise, which did much to solace my sorrow at the loss of my darling Comte and his equally dear son – not to mention all my other good friends at the Château C. But I was young and just starting to feel the full powers of my Lust – and there were so many willing Engines of Consolation about me.

The idea of the place was that, for their subscription, the members had the right to Enjoy two Girls of their choice each week. They could not save up more than four ... oh, well, I won't go into all of the rules; only Men could have dreamed them up. Anything they Desired over that they bought as in any normal House of Pleasure. Each could introduce one guest for one night each month, who then had the freedom of his tool and purse as long as the capacity of either might last. I'll save you the indulgence of your obsession with numbers to say that gave each of us seven girls, on average, the chance of ten guaranteed Occasions of Pleasure each week – plus

188

as many Falls from Grace as our Charms could seduce out of them and their guests.

Still pandering to your fascination with Quantity: I know every member there rogered me in the first week, and most of them twice; also that almost every monthly guest tasted my Favours, too, however many or few of the others he chose. Thus I Enjoyed the Service of some four hundred fine, lusty Gentlemen in all during my year in that place – on top of which, if I may use the phrase, the *regular* Adoration of the Members, which was some twenty Engagements each week – say, eight hundred in that year. The rest is simple Long Division (which was another name for the four-legged frolic which I forgot from those lists I sent you): twelve hundred in a year of, say, two hundred and eighty available days, is between four and five each day. And that, for a Lady of Pleasure who Loves to give her All to each, is a prime number.

In those first weeks, though, when I was the New Sensation of London, and Invitations to the club were as sought after as any that Lady Ell–e later gave out for those same rooms, I was Engaging with more than thrice that number every day. To be sure, sweet little Miss Laycock had endured such a long and delicious rest, she was ready now for All Comers; she drank them up as Sahara does the rain. But such Ravening Greed and Delight could not pass without comment. And one thing led to another, the way they do, and at some stage I must have said, 'Go on – I could take on the lot of you!'

I never meant it to be entered in the Betting Book as some kind of Challenge. But once 'twas there – well, what could I do but honour in seriousness a remark I had dropp'd in jest? Especially as the purse was set at four hundred guineas – which I took to my banker the following Monday. It was a close-run thing, mind. I had forgot

189

that the poor old Earl of Ch–r had his neck broke in a romp with me the month before – though that was incidental. (The Committee exonerated me absolutely of all blame for it; indeed, they agreed with me that any man attempting such things with a woman was risking his neck.) But, alas, I had said 'every single member', not 'every capable member' or some such cautionary rigmarole; they were ever so strict with the exact form of a bet. Well – he was paralyzed from the neck down, you see, and they were all sure he could never perform at all. But one look at Miss Laycock and his tool made a wriggle – which caused him to gasp as much as any man there. And then he was up and flying! Naturally, I had to do all the work, but he spent more copiously than any man else; and I think I even had more Pleasure of him than of some of the others.

I would say it all went to my head if it were not so obvious where it truly went. Poor little Miss Laycock, so greedy on Sunday, so woebegone and sore on Monday! I had to think fast what to do, for if I put myself down sick, they would all jab their fingers at me and sneer they had beat me after all in the only Engagement that counted in that Club. That I would never permit. Nor the forfeiture of my hard-earned four hundred guineas.

So, knowing their utter obsession with gambling, I devised a new sort of game for us to play, and one that would leave Miss Laycock in peace for a while. The three youngest members had all left school the previous year and were as fit and lusty as any I'd ever met. I loved it when any of them took me by the arm and asked me if I would Favour them above (for it was a matter of etiquette among us that no Member ever arrogated the Privilege of our Bodies to himself, but made it a humble plea – which every Girl was only too delighted to Grant). And I had taught all three of them a greater skill in Erotic Arts than any of their generation in Town, I should think. So 'twas to them I put my plan.

At first they all demurred, for they still had some last shred of their natural modesty. But I coaxed and wheedled and made extravagant praise of their prowess and, at last, by dint of throwing in several 'Free Rides' when I had recovered, brought them to agreement. And what a Presentation we made of it! One of them had an uncle, a playwright, who got us some limelight for our stage (really, a small dais on which one or other of us Girls would sometimes sing or recite for their Pleasure). And when the moment came, there stood the three of them, their magnificent young bodies, so manly, true, and bold, all gleaming with oil, and I kneeling before them as naked as Eve.

And then, by swift and dextrous movements of my fingers and lips, I soon had them stiff and trembling, hot for release. Then, having worked copiously with oil over all three, marvelling at their heat and wishing I could have any one of them alone upstairs for an hour or three, I took the middle lad into my mouth and the others into my two hands.

Beth, my closest friend among the Girls, had a racing watch – of which there was no shortage in that club, and every fifteen seconds she called out, 'Change!' Then they all moved down one – right-hand to mouth, mouth to left, left to right-hand, and another fifteen-second timing would begin. The rule was, the lads had to keep utterly still from their hips down – they were not to roger me at all. All such movement had to come from me, and I was by then as adept with either hand as my mouth, and, anyway, what with the constant changes, it was anybody's guess as to which lad would spend first.

None of these rules had been explained, but among betting men, as between Men and Women in matters of Lechery, there is an Instinct which supplies all Needs. Before the second change was due, the bets were flying as to which lad would crack first. By the fifth, a thousand guineas rode on that first free flow of milt. At the last it was my most darling lad of all, young David H–y, who gave out a deep, tormented groan and, holding my head tight between his hands, got himself deep in my throat and gave me all. (You should practise this with your thumb, by the way, or a stick of celery, else it will induce a spontaneous nausea which is the last feeling you truly wish for at that time. Do not use a carrot, for it is too *hard* – though no Man would ever thank you for saying so. The trick is to swallow and swallow against the pressure of it, for the swallowing sends ripples down your gorge that overpower its urges to rise. And better still, it is a Special Squeeze a hundred times more enjoyable for your Lover than even the best that Miss Laycock can manage!) My darling David spent so copiously in me that in the end I laughed and coughed – fortunately so, too, for it gave the betting men the proof whose lack would have led to many a steward's inquiry and perhaps a rerun of the race.

(Which reminds me – talking of stewards. You asked why a Punishment from the steward at the Maison Q. was held in such abject fear by Ladies who might be thought to enjoy such a thing. And you are right, I did forget to tell you. Well, 'twas the other way about. The man was so tender and loving of what he thought were poor, abused lasses, he never plied the stick harder than a tickle anyway!)

Those Who'll-Spend-First races proved so popular I had to rerun the course (with fresh volunteers – who now needed no promise of Free Rides from me) every night that week – and then every Sunday thereafter. The other Girls were at first disgusted and angry, but when they saw what general increase in Traffic it made for them, and all their extra earnings, I was their favourite, too.

But I tell you all this, Sweet Fanny, not in any vaunting sense at all but rather to show you where even the best intentions and the Purest Pursuit of Erotic Bliss can lead: there is something in Men that, once a particular line is started, they must flog it to death. I had started a line in erotic gambling and now it was not enough I should keep it up; but I must invent new Wonders and Spectaculars every week. I would burn with shame now even to mention a half of what my lusty young imagination devised under such encouragement. In my defence I can say it was but a phase I had to go through, like the Maison Q., to know it was something not for me at last. But, being as vigorous and inventive and thorough in it as I was in everything else I did, I have to admit that when the Committee – the Old Men of the club – called me to them and said I had almost destroyed the character of the place, I could not honestly deny it.

There were tears in all our eyes, for we all knew it had been in fun only, and not the slightest harm meant by any of it . . . also we had all of us Enjoyed so many fine rogerings together in privacy above . . . I know how hard it was for them to say I must go. But go I must.

Fortunately, Mrs Featherstonehaugh's Academy was only two streets away. And do you know, the younger members of the Other White's carried me there on a litter in triumph!

And yet I must not boast. No I truly must not, for what I did was very wrong. And it all came about, you see, through my boundless fascination with the possibilities of our erotic nature – the sort of curiosity that now dis-

193

turbs me so much in you, with your endless questions on topics like that.

So there. Sweet Fanny, I have brought myself back to the Academy, where I began this string of epistles. To be sure I have not told you a tenth of my adventures, yet I hope I have told you enough to guide your choice. The rest you must learn for yourself. There is a profound and lovely mystery at the heart of those Pleasures a Man and a Woman can conjure up between themselves; even now I feel I have barely scratched its surface – in my life I mean, for I have certainly done no more than scratch it in these letters to you. Perhaps you, who start so far ahead of me in the game – by the help of my Experience – may plumb it for the world. You will do mankind a greater service than all the religious who ever lived, who only live to cramp the human spirit and plunge it into their alternate orgies of blood, repression, and greed for gold. And do not let the world's opinions sway you. For the fact that a Woman may also be a Lady of Pleasure and be paid for her part in it has no significance. If she loves her Body truly, and loves the Men that Worship it, she has ten thousand times more chance than her chaste sisters to discover the Final Secret of it all.

I have Loved some of the finest Men in Europe in that search. I have had more pleasure of them than Solomon found with his thousand wives. Yet even now I can tremble and shiver with Lust at the thought of one more Encounter – as ardently as at my first! Why?

There's my mystery: Why?

Now – to practical things. Are you coming here in July? And may I prepare François to be your Lover and Guide? Of *course* he is a kind of half-step-uncle to you; I had not in the least forgot it. But if I can romp with him still, step-son and -mother though we may be, then surely you can swallow so small a scruple as that?

Answer me soon for I must prepare another if you will not.

Ever yours, sweet nymph,
Frances
Comtesse de C.

LETTER THIRTEEN

FROM MOUNT VENUS,
Sunday, 30th June 1850

BITCH,

Minx! Hoyden!! Traitress!!! You are no Woman – you are worse than a very Whore!!!! Now, indeed, I see why you were so curious in all those unwomanly questions. Did I not say I could more easily understand it had such interest come from a man? And now, it seems, they did! I was right – oh, yes, I have an unerring instinct in these things. Why did I not trust it? Because I trusted you instead, you . . . you . . . you little Viper in our Bosom. In the bosom of our family.

And who, pray, is this Mr Jeremy Raines who supposes he can make himself a fortune out of publishing my private correspondence with you? (And surely there never was a correspondence between grandmother and granddaughter more private since the invention of writing itself!) How *dare* he? And how dare you show it him without my leave – which, naturally, I should never have given? What is the situation between you and him that you can feel yourself free to share even one page . . . one paragraph . . . one *word* of matters so intimate as I have described for you?

Yes, 'twas all for YOU, my once-Sweet Fanny, my once-so-Darling Grandchild. Oh I could weep every tear from my eye when I think of my hopes for you. I wrote it all for you. 'Twas no heavy chore, I grant; indeed, I accept I wrote it all with Relish. But nine-tenths of my Pleasure was the knowing I shared it with you alone. With every Lascivious and Voluptuary memory, as it returned to me, I thought of you – believing that one day soon you would be dancing to that same mysterious melody of our Desires. When I described myself and the Comte in the sweet hours of my Initiation, I saw you lying in my dear, sweet François' embrace, writhing with your Pleasure, moaning your astonishment that such Delights had lain hidd'n in your adorable Young Body, unused and unsuspected all this time. When I portrayed myself driving away after my night on HMS D. (which was only one out of *dozens* of such Passages of Pleasure I might have chosen to describe) I pictured you doing the same – and with your dear little *cutte* still glowing at the Ardent Adoration of so many fine, upstanding Men.

And now you have cast it all aside! You have thrown it back in my face! You have turned my dreams and memories to ashes in my mouth! You are that ignorant merchant who cast away a Pearl, richer than all his tribe. Very well – make your filthy fortune! Or let Mr Jeremy

Raines make his – for I hope you don't imagine he'll truly share it with you, do you? You will learn soon enough that money does not bring happiness. The only true joys you will ever know will all come in through your Tail. You fool! I could have taught you to wag that Tail and increase your Joys a thousandfold over what any run-of-the-mill young woman might expect – *and* have made a fortune out of it, too – enough to leave your filthy publisher gasping with dismay.

Well, so be it. You have made your bed. Now lie in it. You are no more granddaughter of mine. And you may join your dear mother in the waiting room for Hell!

Priez d'accepter, Mademoiselle, mes Sentiments les plus Respectables,

Frances
Comtesse de C.

PS In any case, you have gone off at half-cock. Or your Mr Jeremy Raines has done – how like a Man! What have I given you so far? Some juvenile experiments in Erotic Pleasure; one night in an Officers' Mess; and a few incidents so perverse and foul no *normal* Man could read of them with any Joy at all! What a fine trawl you have made yourselves! Why, I have a thousand times as much stored away in Memory's Vaults – which, had you played your hand better, you could have wheedled from me while François made a Woman of you and the cream of the French nobility taught you all the Joys of Venus and showered you with gold! 'Twould have made your Readers *drool* at the mouth. And you have let it all go by you! So the last laugh is mine.

PPS Better still! *I* shall write those Memoirs you did not know you scorned! They will scorch the page. Yes! I have no little Talent for it, don't you think? They will be so Hot that what I gave *you* will be as icebergs in a frozen sea; the Public will hurl them back in your faces. Ha ha! You shall not make a penny after all!

PPPS Perhaps you think I boast? You may suspect that after I left Mrs Featherstonehaugh's my path was the traditional one whereby Lady of Pleasure turns Whore? You see a steady downward path from knocking shop to Drury Lane to St Katherine's dock? You see me, a poor drunken wretch, tumbling foreign sailors in the gutter . . . at last discovered by the Comte, my first, my only, my one True Love . . . and so rescued and restored to my present health, a Penitent at last? Eh? That would be the way of it if your clever Publisher schemed it out, I'm sure. A stirring tale of Lust and Depravity for a thousand pages, all swiftly wrapped up in a final paragraph of Discovery and Moral Restitution. Very pretty! Then, mademoiselle, I have the honour to inform you that when the Comte again came into my life at the still-tender age of thirty-two (he being then a mere stripling sixty, and horny as ever) the situation was thus: The dress on my back had cost one of my paramours over one hundred pounds; I had a villa in the Bois de Boulogne; a Box at the Opéra; two dozen servants indoors; a chef (Fleur, in fact) who made my table the cynosure of every *bon vivand* in Paris; and the Comte and I met on the threshold of the office of the most important minister of the day, where the Attraction of my Charms had just proved powerful enough to thrust aside all matters of State (except the fevered state of his tool) for a whole hour! What happened between Mrs Featherstonehaugh's and there shall be the subject of *my* book. So rush yours out, you little fools, while you yet have time. It is but a summer weed with a few short days to bloom!

LETTER FOURTEEN

FROM MOUNT VENUS,
Friday, 12th July 1850

Sweet Fanny,

Perhaps I was too hasty, after all. I feared Mr Jeremy Raines had got there before us and spoiled you for Life – for François would never have considered you without your Jewel intact, you know. But you really should have explained to me he was of *that* persuasion. Did you think I should be shocked! Sweet Fanny, I have induced as many of them to understand they might Enjoy the occasional Love of a Woman as I have taught young Girls, who thought they were made but to enjoy Men, to find a now-and-then Rapture with one another. 'Tis the same Flesh, the same Lust, the same Jig, and the same Ecstasy at the end of it all.

You should also have told me how great an income you expect to derive from the publication of my Tale. ('Twill not be the first time that Commodity – or something sounding very like it – has been published for Sale!) It puts such an entirely different complexion upon everything. And you say he will offer even *more* for the rest? I feel the warmest sentiments toward him already. True, *my* memoirs are just about the most Scorching thing I ever read in that line. I thought Harriet W–n's so-called 'Memoirs' the feeblest thing ever; she was *bored* to death by her Lovers and she then did the same, in the other sense of the term, to the world. When Wellington told *her*, 'Publish and be damn'd!' he spoke a larger truth than he knew.

Cora P–l has shown me some of her scribbling, too; which she hopes to publish when her tipperary fortune has vanished where it came from. My dear, such coyness! And it ill becomes her, who was never better than a vulgar hackney of a Union Street bitch.

Fanny Hill was good enough, though 'twas plainly writ for a more genteel reader – and writ by a Man, to boot, who can never truly understand how it feels to be a Woman, especially at that moment of Bliss when she yields him Her Favour. They believe *they* win us always; little do they know how oft the Triumph is ours!

No, I think we shall sweep them all from the field. The victory is ours already. Speaking of *Victory*, did I tell you that at the age of twenty-one, when I was at the very height of my Sensual Power, I was dined on that vessel – and rogered soon after by the entire Board of Admiralty? There's another one for our book! I must make a note of it now. Oh, there is so much to recall!

Hurry, hurry, do! Your dear François is waiting with pale face and trembling frame now that he has seen the photos you sent. (The one showing your Maidenhead

Intact was a trifle *de trop*, I felt; there will be time enough for proofs of that, and in warmer ambience, too. But 'tis a small chiding. The others are superb.) Mr Raines took them, you say? I begin to have hopes of him. (Do not share this letter with him, for there is nothing here to his interest – every word here is pure as snow.) The way his lens has lingered on your exquisite curves shows at least some understanding of the Lusts of the generality of Men. The very sight of you made poor François' eyes pop out. Your neck and breasts are just perfect. Your waist is a little too trim for modern taste, but then you are so young still. It was the same in my day. Men claimed to admire Women built like Juno – bosoms like bolsters and backsides like a barrel of feathers. But let a little gazelle like me wriggle and squirm all over 'em, all lithe and lissom and slender, and their Junos were all turned to great, sweating mares whose ample folds of lard would engulf their Desire and smother it at birth. No, you will spread untold new Pleasure in the world when you are broken to the Game – and you will get it all back, ten times as much. Oh, does your sweet little *cutte* not already melt and shiver at the prospect? How I envy you. Men are so much cleaner in their persons now. (On the other hand they are less Vicious. There were some fine, inventive spirits abroad when I began!)

What more?

Nothing!

Dear heart, I have run out of things to say! I cannot wait for you to get here and begin your *éducation senti-mentale*. We must write it all down, day by day, exactly as it happens. It would make an entirely complementary book to mine, which are Memoirs and tinted with the rosy forgiveness of time. Yours would be a Diary – the Raw Experience of a Young Girl, filled with shapeless Desires, drowning in Longings she cannot yet discern or name, as she enters for the first time the Wonderland of Erotic Desire and Fulfillment. 'Twould be all urgency, breathlessness, bewilderment ... tears, laughter, joy, pain ... lust and exhaustion and revival. ... and then lust again, and again, and again as the Great God Pan claims her for his tribe and adorns her with the golden Girdle of Erotic Desires she can never finally gratify but must wander the world, eternally seeking her release.

Oh, my dear – we have a new *Industry* here between us!

You will be met by the Comte's coach at C–s and brought straight to Paris, not here. I shall greet you in Paris, and we shall stay at a very Discreet House of Pleasure we own there. We can settle our business with Mr Raines, and then we will buy your entire wardrobe. You shall have gowns and dresses and cloaks for an empress! And nor shall we neglect your underthings, your stockings and garters, your frills and furbelows, your nightdresses and perfumes, and all the spices and creams you'll use as you set the World on Fire with a brand-new Lust for you!

Ever yours, sweet nymph,
Frances
Comtesse de C.

INTRODUCTION

For obvious reasons this 'Introduction' had to be postponed until after the surprises of the final two chapters had been allowed to unfold; it has now become a reluctant *Envoi* instead. But even had these words of mine been in their conventional place, the temptation to head them *Re*introduction would have been overwhelming. It is a rare pleasure, indeed, for someone who has made a lifelong study of erotic literature to be able to restore to our 'locked cabinets' (actually, does anyone bother to lock them any more?) one of the lost masterpieces of the genre in English.

Sweet Fanny had a most tortuous history. It was first published by Jeremy Raines in Kent in 1860, a date whose significance will be clear in a moment. It appears to have been distributed only in England, which is

207

strange since there was, even then, quite a flourishing Continental market for erotic books in English; lovers of such works have always been people of taste and education, so a foreign language was never much of a barrier. It appears that both the Countess and her beloved Comte put down their collective foot and refused to let it be distributed on their side of the Channel.

The Comte was not, of course, the wise, kindly, almost saint-like figure that Fanny gives us in these pages – though he was not without his generous side, either. Those girls who truly pleased him never had the smallest cause to complain of his meanness. But he was, too, one of the shrewdest and hardest-headed sexual entrepreneurs in that most sexually entrepreneurial age and country: nineteenth-century France. His family fortunes were left in ruins after the revolution, the Château and its estates encumbered with debt; but from that inauspicious beginning, with nothing but his own unbridled lechery to guide him, he built up the largest 'sex empire', as we would now call it, in the world.

When he met Fanny again in 1832 (and the location, the outer office of the President of the Republic, seems genuine), he was desperately in need of a 'super-madam' to take over the management of some of his *maisons tolérées*. (The two such places that Fanny off-handedly admits to owning in these pages were the merest fraction of the total.) In 1830 the Comte had rashly opened a number of Houses in which all the girls were aged between fourteen and nineteen. They were extremely popular with their clientèle but the problems of managing girls of that tempestuously emotional age had almost defeated him. His old flame, with her by now vast experience, exactly fitted the bill. No doubt they had once been in love, or as much in love as two such sexually voracious people ever can be; and perhaps it had survived. It certainly seems to have *re*vived, for they lived happily together in their various mansions and châteaux until the Comte died (with, as she coyly records, *un certain sourire* on his lips) in his ninetieth year in 1860.

Plainly, while he lived, *Sweet Fanny* could not be published. Even then, it appears, the entire project was carried out against the most bitter opposition from the newly widowed Countess. Something of her enormous power can be gauged from the fact that Raines did not dare distribute the book outside Britain; and even there she meddled and connived to such effect that the number of copies actually sold was derisory. No government, with all the power of the law behind it, has ever been so successful as Fanny at suppressing a work of this quality. Out of a printing of 500, some 473 copies were seized in the infamous Customs raid on Raines's home in Deal on February 14th, 1869. Still, that ought to have left 27 in circulation.

And here the mystery (or the evidence of the Countess's enormous power) deepens. The burning of those 473 copies received widespread notices. *Sweet Fanny* was suddenly, in every sense, a hot property. The usual result of such hamfisted attempts to suppress any work of erotic literature is to give it a cachet far beyond its merits; the remaining copies come out of the woodwork and new pirated editions are run off by the thousand to cash in on the temporary notoriety. But no such thing seems to have happened with this particular masterpiece.

In Fanny's own memoirs, which have not been published but which her descendants have kindly permitted me to see, there is just a hint of a cause for this strange silence. First she describes how Raines, having secretly printed 500 copies of the work ('It was all his fiction,' she asserted self-righteously, 'for he so heavily rewrote my originals that no trace of me remained . . .'), tried to sell

209

them clandestinely, one at a time, to his richest and most discreet clients. And then she dismisses the entire subject with the words: 'But we saw him off.'

In the light of what happened, this can only mean that all 27 copies that poor Raines imagined he had sold to his favoured clients *were, in fact, bought by agents of the Countess!* Perhaps, too, it was she who tipped the Customs men off? Significantly enough, it was a special squad that came down with a box of matches from London to do the job; Raines had always enjoyed the most cordial relations with the local men, whose matches suffered dreadfully from the damp sea breezes. Until her death in 1900 (she was right about seeing her century out), she always maintained that every copy of 'Raines's fiction' had been destroyed. And when, after the most assiduous search in all the likely places in Europe and America, not a single copy turned up, it was not unnaturally assumed that she somehow knew what she was talking about.

It is all the more extraordinary, then, to relate that the copy from which this present edition is taken turned up in Leningrad during the years when that city lay under siege by the German army in the Second World War! It was rescued by a man, now dead, whom I shall (at the request of his family) call 'Vladimir'. He was a lecturer at the university there and had an excellent command of English. If he had not happened to be walking down a certain street, just off the Nevsky Prospekt, on a particularly bitter afternoon in the January of 1943 – in the final days of the siege – the world would have lost this masterpiece for ever. By that time everything consumable in that brave city had been eaten and everything burnable burned. An old peasant from far off in the country, who had been trapped in the city by the speed of the German advance some fifteen months earlier, was throwing the last of his possessions into a street brazier in an attempt to

210

conjure up some warmth. Among them were two ikons – which was evidence enough of the sort of desperation that had seized people there. Vladimir, moved by the man's distress – and distressed enough himself at such vandalism, however understandable – stopped him and bought the precious relics on the spot.

The word 'ikon' conjures up a picture of the Virgin and Child, painted hundreds of years ago, and now worth a fortune. Sometimes, if you're lucky, it is; but the Russian peasant can make an ikon of anything. In his memoirs *The Vanished Pomps of Yesterday*, published in several editions from the 1890s onward, Lord Frederic Hamilton describes a bear hunt he attended in the hinterland around St Petersburg (as Leningrad was formerly called). He left behind a razor and shaving brush, and when he returned the following year he discovered that the peasants, on whom he was once again billeted, had turned the two items into an ikon. They had put them in an old cigar box, onto whose lid they had then daubed a hamfisted representation of the Madonna and Child.

And it was an identical process that had led to the preservation of this particular copy of *Sweet Fanny*! Poor Vladimir had no idea what to do with his find! He could hardly disclose it to his superiors, for, like all repressive regimes, the Soviet government took a dim view of erotic pleasures in any of their forms. The 'ikon' hung around the family apartment for years – until, in fact, last year (1987), when I happened to be in Leningrad doing some tricky but enjoyable on-the-spot reasearch into prostitution in the city (where, as all the government handouts tell you, it doesn't even exist). Word of my inquiries reached Vladimir's son, a colonel in the KGB, and he sent for me as only a man in that exalted position can. What followed is not especially relevant to this present work, so let us just say that 'after negotiations of a protracted nature,' the book – the last remaining copy on earth of this legendary masterpiece – passed into my hands. And my other researches were also magically assisted.

The book itself – my copy of it, I mean – gives only the most tantalizing hint of its provenance. There is, naturally, no name or bookplate – and certainly no bookseller's ticket. But an obviously Victorian hand has written on the flyleaf: 'FH 23, Ld G 19, R St E 44, WH 22,' followed by the assertion: 'FH owes me 4gns.'

The figures are probably scores in some kind of card game. The fact that the words were English led me to investigate the British community of St Petersburg during the 1860s – beginning, of course, with the embassy, since that is where expatriate life would have found its centre. I had little hope of turning up anything at all relevant, however – and so was nearly bowled over to discover, within the first hour, that Lord Frederic Hamilton and one Ralph St Erskine had been on the embassy staff during that time! The former rose to the rank of Second Secretary by the time he left; the latter was in Chancery. 'Ld G' and 'WH' had no obvious counterparts (and it is not the first time in the history of literature that the initials 'WH' have proved elusive!) but they were probably 'expats' living in the city.

It was this clue that led me to read Lord Frederic's autobiography, where I came across his story of the razor-and-shaving-brush ikon; until then I had not even half believed Vladimir's son when he told me that *Fanny* had been ikonized in that way.

The net was closed tighter still when, in Fanny's unpublished memoirs, in the volumes that deal with the sixties, she mentions young Ralph St Erskine as an occasional visitor, with a hint that he was a suitor of her granddaughter, Young Fanny, as I will call her. I am not at liberty to describe the context as yet. Negotiations are now in progress that, I hope, will lead ultimately to the publication of Fanny's autobiography in full and under my editorship; but from what she says about the young man it is plain that, if any copies of the book had been lying around their mansions or châteaux, one of them would certainly have stuck to R St E. But let us not chide him, Gentle Reader, for, had he been as honest as the day, this most improbable chain of circumstance would never have been forged, and then neither you nor I would today be able to enjoy what our great-grandfathers would have given their teeth to possess.

Fanny's shrill and oft-repeated assertion that Raines had so drastically edited and rewritten her original letters to her granddaughter force us to ask how much truth there might be in her protestations. (But at least she never denied having written *something* to the girl – and of a highly incandescent nature, at that.) Unfortunately I was not allowed sufficient time with her memoirs to make a point-by-point comparison; also, I was not then suffi- ciently confident of the family's good intentions even to admit I had a copy of *Sweet Fanny* in my possession; so we are forced to turn to the text itself for whatever clues it may offer.

Even from a cursory reading it is obvious that our Fanny has *some* cause for complaint. Erotic Novels are a strict sort of genre; if they do not deliver what their readers expect, they do not sell. And among the things that readers expect are: a vivacious and pretty young heroine, eager for experience; a First Time that leaves her stunned by her own sensuality and eager for more-more-more; the growth in her of a voracious and unsatisfiable lust; some hedonistic lesbianism and troilism; a brief sojourn in deviant territory (flagellation and pederasty, for instance);

213

her own happy seduction of a virgin youth; and (in Victorian times) a final chapter in which, with blatant insincerity, she Repents of it All.

Except for this latter requirement (which is, I believe, a significant departure), *Sweet Fanny* gives us the lot. Her tireless (not to say tire*some*) Comte and her equally untiring cunt are both, clearly, features of pure male fantasy. So is the pat sequence of events as she unfolds them to us. And yet I cannot help feeling, especially when I compare it with other erotic novels of the 1860s, that, try as he might to homogenize our Fanny and reduce her to the status of the conventional porno-queen of that day, poor old Raines was on a hiding to nothing. A thread of joyful, joyous truth has somehow survived it all. There actually lived an irreducible, irrepressible young woman called Fanny Dale, whose appetite for sex was, indeed, enormous and who cut a lustful swathe through Regency London almost as catastrophic as the one 'she' describes here – and *Raines simply could not shake her off.*

We, in our sophistication – our determination not to swallow all that old male fantasy stuff – must beware of falling into the opposite trap: of assuming that all whores are frigid man-haters none of whom is even capable of feeling affection for a client, much less of climaxing with him. Even as I write these words, there is a documentary on the television in which a prostitute, identified only as 'Vicki', says: 'All punters imagine they make me come. Well, some do and some don't – and whether they do or not has nothing to do with them. It's all down to what side you got out of bed that morning . . . what sort of a day you've had . . . and the number you first thought of. And I would not go two feet out of my way to enjoy a physical thrill. That's how unimportant it is to me.' Now that, to me, has the ring of honesty.

The alternative view was well described by the Russian

214

writer Alexander Kuprin, whose 1914 novel *Yama: The Pit* was a brutal and realistic exposé of life in a two-rouble brothel in Moscow during the first decade of this century. (Some have called it the *Uncle Tom's Cabin* of *white* slavery.) All Kuprin's whores feel an utter, 'almost squeamish' indifference to men – except poor Pasha, a 'sad, peculiar girl' who was 'afflicted with the most dreadful nymphomania'. The other girls despised her when they heard her abandoned cries and moans of pleasure with each and every client; she ought to have been locked up in an asylum, they said.

Pasha is a product of that other male fantasy: the need to appear strong and to soar above all gentle feelings. In creating Pasha, Kuprin seems to be pleading: 'Listen – I know I'm writing about whores and therefore thinking about them all day long . . . also describing lots of sexy things they get up to . . . but *I'm* not taken in by it all! Oh no – I still know where to draw the moral line. Just look at my Pasha if you doubt it.'

Somewhere between the two male fantasies lies the truth; and *Our Fanny*, no matter how heavily filtered through Raines's editorial talent and the demands of the genre, points to it – and reveals it to be a profounder truth than either fantasy could claim.

Take away everything that Raines added, and I think we are still left with a lovely, pert, vivacious, and alto-gether splendid woman. Raines knew it, too. After all, he actually met her, and, although she was in her fifties by then, time had not dimmed those particular qualities in her. I'm sure that is why – against all his better instincts as a pornographer – he left us so much of the original Fanny, intact (if that is not altogether too bizarre a word to use of her!).

Thank heavens he did.

* * *

But that is not the last of his gifts to us. I said that Vladimir rescued *two* ikons. The second was none other than *Fanny's Diary* – the very diary that, in the final chapters of this present book, Fanny urges her young granddaughter to keep. I did not even know that Young Fanny had complied with the suggestion, much less published the resulting manuscript. The only evidence we had of her existence – at all – was that contained here in the pages of *Sweet Fanny*. Whether she had ever gone to France, or met François and been deflowered by him, was a matter of absolute conjecture.

I am now (Gentle Reader will be delighted to know) preparing this new and hitherto quite unknown masterpiece for the press, so I shall say no more of substance here – beyond this: Young Fanny did, indeed, go to France – and she looked forward keenly to trying out everything her grandmother had suggested. But from the moment she set foot in Europe, everything went wrong. She was, however – every sweet and adorable inch of her – a worthy offspring of the marvellous Lady of Pleasure we have already met.

And that, finally, brings me to a prospect even more dazzling. For, in the few, brief hours during which I was permitted to browse among the family archives, I found evidence of *yet another* Fanny, herself a granddaughter to the one I have to call Young Fanny here. She served as a nurse in Flanders during the First World War – where, entirely without lascivious prompting from any of her female forebears, she seems to have discovered that joyful obsession with carnal pleasure that had ruled the lives of Fanny and Young Fanny alike.

Does it surface every other generation? Is there even now, as you read these words, a Fanny of the 1980s who is just being knocked off her feet by the discovery of sex – and so beginning her own unbreakable addiction to

216

what her great-great-great-great-grandmother, our own beloved Fanny, called the Gay Old Life?

If you're out there, darling Fanny the Fourth, and if by any chance you happen to read these words . . . do please get in touch! To paraphrase a remark of your sainted forebear: 'We could have a whole new Industry here between us!'

Faye Rossignol
Maidenhead
1988

Headline books are available at your bookshop or newsagent, or can be ordered from the following address:

Headline Book Publishing PLC
Cash Sales Department
PO Box 11
Falmouth
Cornwall
TR10 9EN
England

UK customers please send cheque or postal order (no currency), allowing 60p for postage and packing for the first book, plus 25p for the second book and 15p for each additional book ordered up to a maximum charge of £1.90 in UK.

BFPO customers please allow 60p for postage and packing for the first book, plus 25p for the second book and 15p per copy for the next seven books, thereafter 9p per book.

Overseas and Eire customers please allow £1.25 for postage and packing for the first book, plus 75p for the second book and 28p for each subsequent book.